DANGEROUS CHRISTMAS INHERITANCE

JANDA SAMPLE

Cover design by 100 Covers.

Created with Vellum

To my mom and Jeanne, who would have bought the first two copies, if not the first ten. I love and miss you both so much.

To my writers' group. This book would not have happened without you. And I mean that in the most literal way possible.

And to my dad, who said this story was, "not bad."

PROLOGUE

The two houses couldn't have been more different from each other.

One was brightly lit. Warmth and comfort shined through the windows, and Christmas lights danced across the roof line. A wreath hung neatly on the door and snow drifts piled against the windows. Just looking at the house, you could almost smell the Christmas cookies and hear the carols playing.

The other house was dark. The lit lamps created more shadows than light. Decorations sat in boxes in the living room, pushed aside and forgotten. You could smell the cigarette smoke and hear the heated words.

Both houses played with the memories of a little girl, and although she loved the first house, she lived in the second.

CHAPTER 1

Kate Sinclair lay flat on her back with arms and legs akimbo in the middle of the floor. Every imaginable type of old-fashioned Christmas décor surrounded her, forming a red and green papier-mâché version of a crime scene body outline, which seemed appropriate because Kate was fairly certain this Christmas was going to kill her. Why had she decided to do this? What had possessed her to pay a neighbor's son to load up his wagon with boxes labeled "Christmas" in what she assumed was her grandmother's handwriting, make three trips from her house to her restoration and antiques shop, and dump the boxes in a pile next to the register counter? Now she was spending the Monday after Thanksgiving emptying all the boxes in some vague semblance of organizing and sorting.

She was tired, her back hurt, and she still had to clean everything up before opening tomorrow. Her dog, Jupiter, barked as a tap-tap-tap echoed through the store. She tried to roll her head back to determine where the sound came from, but a cardboard box tipped precariously towards her and blocked her line of sight. The tap turned to a knock.

"Kate? Are you okay?" A voice called from the glass door at the front of her shop.

She sat up and shoved the menacing box more securely into place with one hand, raising the other hand over her head in a wave at the glass door behind her. The UPS man had arrived. "Give me a second." She grimaced. He would have something to say about this mess. She made her way to the door, stepping gingerly over ribbons and bows, trying not to trip over creches and ornaments. Unlocking the door and pushing it open, she gave him a smile. "Welcome to Santa's workshop." She kicked aside some fake greenery to make room for him to walk inside.

He gave Jupiter a pat on the head. "Hey, boy. What's going on in here?" He looked up at Kate. "It's like Christmas blew up."

"That's the best you've got?"

"Well, you were sprawled on the ground like you'd barely survived an atomic explosion."

"That sounds about right." She eyed the box in his hand. "Just one today?"

"Yep." He set the box on the counter and made a note on his tablet. "So, um, are you all right?"

Heat rose in her cheeks. "I must look like a mess, but yeah, I'm fine. Just dealing with some... stuff."

"So that's what you call this."

Kate turned and surveyed the mess. "It all belonged to my grandmother. I've been ignoring the boxes since I moved into her house, but apparently Christmas is coming back again this year, so I thought I'd finally take the time to go through everything. I brought the boxes here in case there were some antiques or interesting items I could sell." She pointed over her shoulder. "And there's a dumpster out back for the rest."

"Or you could use the decorations to, I don't know, decorate?"

"Oh, now you're going to start on me too?"

He picked up a strand of garland and wrapped it around his

neck. Tossing the end over his shoulder, he affected his best southern accent, "Why, whatever do you mean?"

Kate laughed. "I heard the whispers loud and clear last year. I know people were beside themselves about my Christmas decorations."

"I think you mean your lack of Christmas decorations."

"I decorated."

"You printed out a sign that said 'Merry Christmas' and taped it to the front door."

"That's decorating."

"You didn't even use colored ink."

Kate rolled her eyes. "Fair point. But I had only recently moved here and had just opened the shop. There was a lot going on."

"That was your saving grace. People gave you the benefit of the doubt. If you don't decorate this year, there may be a lynch mob."

"Why do people care?" She really didn't understand the fuss this town made about Christmas.

"Decorating for Christmas is a rite of passage in Hemingway. It's a badge of honor. You've got a storefront on a busy, public street. It's your civic duty to make this place festive."

Kate sighed. "Fine. Not that I don't have better things to do with my time, but I will put up some decorations."

"I like that you used the plural form of the word. It's a good start. And with that, I'll leave you to it." He gave Jupiter a quick scratch behind the ears, then headed for the door, tiptoeing through the floor decor like it was a minefield. "See you tomorrow."

Kate opened her mouth to remind him he was still wearing a garland scarf, but the door had already closed behind him. She shook her head and smiled. After a year of small-talk and jokes, she really should learn his name.

❄

THREE HOURS LATER, KATE HAD THE STORE MORE ORGANIZED, IF not more empty. She had several piles for the dumpster, a collection of items to sell, a group of items to refurbish before selling, and even a small pile of items to use for decorating the shop. If she took the trash out, the store would be clean enough for customers tomorrow. She grabbed two trash bags off the top of the heap, knocking a box down. It landed on its side, the contents spilling out onto the floor.

Kate groaned. The goal was to clean up the trash, not make a bigger mess. She glanced back to see what spilled out of the box, hoping it wasn't the remnants of lunch. Thankfully, the box had only held several cardboard houses that had been part of a rather cheap-looking Christmas village. She hefted the bags higher in her hands and walked to the back door but paused before pushing it open. Something about those houses had caught her attention the first time she sorted through the decorations. Setting the bags down, she looked at the houses scattered across the floor. They were falling apart and, yes, they were cardboard, obviously trash. But something about them tugged at her memory—nothing specific, but definitely a deja vu feeling. Of what, she didn't know. Maybe she'd seen something similar at a flea market or another store.

She walked to one of the houses and picked it up, turning it in her hands. Small scraps of greenery and whiffs of cotton were glued around hand-drawn windows. Pieces of bark made up the roof and baby blue wallpaper wrapped around the house as rough siding. If she had seen similar villages in other stores, maybe they were worth more than she'd originally thought. They were cute, in a homeless cardboard shack kind of way. She picked up the other houses and gently placed them back in the box alongside several other small town buildings. Maybe she should research them a bit before tossing them. In the meantime, it wouldn't be a horrible idea to fix them up a little and display them in the window, as some of those Christmas decorations everyone was so obsessed with.

CHAPTER 2

Kate looked up from her computer at the sound of the bell above her door. Jupiter lifted his head and barked.

"Be right out."

"Take your time—it's just me." Kate recognized the voice of the UPS man. "But I do have pizza and it's still hot."

"In that case, I'm coming right now!" She left her office and walked into the main room of her store.

"So without the pizza, you would've kept me waiting?"

"I said no such thing. Why are you bringing pizza into my shop?"

"Tony's had a two-for-one sale today, so naturally, I had to get two. I mean, that's just good finances. But since I can't eat two, and I know you usually sustain yourself with little more than a Pop-Tart, I brought you one. Have you eaten?"

"You mean besides the Pop-Tart? No. Thank you, this is really nice of you."

"No worries. Although, I kept the free one, so you owe me $8.25."

She laughed. "Put it on my tab."

He looked at the counter, searching for a place to set the pizza box. "Can I move these?" He motioned to the cardboard village spread out across the counter.

"Oh, sorry." Kate slid the buildings out of the way.

"They're, um... cute?"

Kate laughed, "They're a mess."

He swiped the back of his hand across his forehead in mock relief. "I was worried you didn't know that. What are they?"

"It's a Christmas village my grandmother had in those boxes from yesterday."

He set the pizza on the counter and pushed Jupiter's nose away. "Sorry, Jup, not for you." He picked up one of the dilapidated houses. "I thought your grandmother was rich. Why does her Christmas village look like a kindergarten craft project?"

"Maybe it was a kindergarten craft project. Maybe my dad made it when he was little. Although I was just doing a little research online and came up with another option. Apparently, back before ceramic villages became popular in the '70s, people would make these elaborate village scenes and putz around with them throughout the Christmas season, adding pieces, moving them around, rearranging them. So they called them putz houses."

"Seriously?"

"Yep. They'd usually start with a nativity scene and build out from there. As you can see, similar sizing and time periods weren't a big concern. They kind of took on a life of their own, I guess."

"It's just cardboard, but since it's old cardboard," he set down the house, "does that mean they're valuable?"

"Not just cardboard. Don't overlook the newspaper, sticks, rocks and, quite honestly, trash. They don't appear to be worth too much, but I'm still doing research. I was about to throw them in the dumpster yesterday, but I rescued them at the last minute. I thought I might use them for a window display."

"Speaking of which, I'm impressed." He pointed towards the garland she'd hung from the ceiling with ball ornaments attached. "You actually put up some decorations."

Kate dipped her head, pleased he'd noticed her meager attempt at decorating. "I didn't want anyone throwing eggs at the windows."

"Smart decision. Now I can use my eggs for something more useful, like egg salad or an omelet." He picked up a small steepled building. "I think putting these in the window is a great idea. You've got a church, a couple of businesses, a few houses. You could make a nice little Christmas scene. I think your customers would get a kick out of it. Although that house needs a little something." He nodded to the only house without any decorations. Little bits of dried glue stuck to the cardboard, evidence of previous decorations now long gone.

"I could just throw that one away."

"Or you decorate it."

"Or I could leave it undecorated."

"But then it looks so sad."

"Why is it sad?"

"There's no color. It's a dark house."

Kate leaned her hip against the counter and crossed her arms. "So? Maybe they can't afford decorations."

He mimicked her stance, facing her. "And that would be sad."

"Or maybe they just don't have time."

"Yeah, that's sad too."

She pushed away from the counter and walked around to the other side. "Oh good grief. Maybe they just don't like decorations."

He frowned. "That's the saddest reason of all."

"That's not sad! Why is that sad?"

"I get it." He plucked the dark house from its place on the counter, bouncing it slightly in his hand as he looked at her. "You have a dark, undecorated house, don't you?"

Kate snatched the house from his hand and set it down next to the other buildings. "Look, not decorating a house is a personal choice. Maybe the owner's Jewish, or they prefer to just decorate the inside so they can appreciate their handiwork. Or maybe they prefer to not deal with the aggravation. Just because someone chooses not to decorate doesn't mean there's something wrong with them."

He held up a hand in front of him. "Whoa, I never said there was anything wrong with them. I'm sorry, I didn't mean to touch a nerve."

"You didn't touch a nerve. I just think this town is a little too obsessed with Christmas."

"Hey, no worries. I should mind my own business. Besides, I've got packages to deliver, so I should get to it. You got anything going out for me?"

Kate shook her head. "Not today. I should have a few going out tomorrow, though."

"Sure thing." He gave a quick nod and headed for the door.

"Thanks for the pizza," she called after him.

He nodded again, holding the door open for two women as they entered the store.

Kate smiled at them as she put the pizza and her dog into the back office. "Hello, welcome to Out of the Attic."

THE WOMEN LEFT, HAPPY WITH THEIR PURCHASES, AND KATE opened the pizza box to grab a now-cold slice. It really was nice of him to bring it. Had she overreacted about the dark house? Maybe she owed him an apology. Jupiter came and laid his head on her lap, and she absently rubbed his velvety ears.

She had a weird relationship with the UPS guy. He'd been delivering packages to her since she'd opened the store a little over a year ago, and they often joked with each other and exchanged small talk. Not quite a friendship but more than acquaintances. They knew nothing personal about each other. Still, she looked forward to his visits. He made her laugh, and they had an easy rapport. But it was horrible that she didn't know his name. He knew hers because it was on the packages he delivered, but they'd never officially introduced themselves. By the time it dawned on her that she should ask his name, she was too embarrassed she hadn't already. Maybe she should just ask the next time she saw him. He could get two apologies for the price of one.

HAVING DECIDED TO PUT THE PUTZ VILLAGE IN THE WINDOW display, Kate gathered the buildings together. Each was three to six inches wide, and while not heavy, it could be cumbersome to carry several at once. But never being the type of person to make two trips when she could manage one, Kate piled the buildings in her arms and headed towards the window. Her black shadow of a dog lay in the corner, watching her, but as she rounded the counter, he stood and rushed towards her, his tail wagging frantically.

"Jupiter, no!" He skidded to a stop, bumping into her legs. She tried to come to an equally sudden stop but was less successful. She flung her arms out to steady herself, the buildings she had been carrying raining down on Jupiter. He yelped and ran behind the counter. "Oh Jup, I'm sorry!" She leaned over the counter to look at him. "Are you okay? I'm sorry. Come here. You're alright."

Jupiter cowered in the corner, but came when she called. He stood on his hind legs and put his front paws on the counter. Kate rubbed his head, paying special attention to his ears. His tail wagged and he licked her hands. "See, you're okay. Good boy, Jup."

She turned to inspect the damage done to the village, looking down at the buildings dropped haphazardly by her feet. Most of them looked no worse for the wear, but one of the houses had lost its roof. She picked up the two pieces. She could glue the roof back on pretty easily, but one of the inside walls seemed damaged too. She looked closer. It wasn't damaged. What had looked like a tear was actually a pocket of sorts taped onto the inside wall.

She peered more closely, then turned the house upside down and gave it a shake. A small key dropped into her hand, too small for a house or car. Even too small for a safety deposit box. It looked like it might belong to an old luggage lock. She slipped the key into her pocket. Maybe there was something in the attic at home that the key would fit. She gave her dog another pat on the head and went in search of glue to fix the roofless putz house.

AT THE SOUND OF KNOCKING ON THE WINDOW, KATE LOOKED UP from arranging snow around the buildings to see an older gentleman staring at the village from the sidewalk. He made a motion towards the village and seemed to ask a question, but she had no idea what he said. She pointed to the door and walked towards it. She barely had the door opened when he pushed his way in, heading straight to the window display.

"Hello." She spoke to his back. "How are you this evening?"

He didn't even glance in her direction. "I'd like to buy this Christmas village."

Kate bristled at his peremptory tone. "It's not for sale at the moment."

"When will it be for sale?"

"I'm not sure. Honestly, maybe never."

He jerked his head from the display to her. His white, bushy eyebrows met in a V as he narrowed his eyes. "Then why put it in the window?"

"To decorate for Christmas. I was told people around here like that kind of thing."

He smirked. "Yes, they do. And so do I. Specifically this village. You can name your price."

She really needed to do more research on the value of these putz things. "Out of curiosity, why are you so interested in the village?"

"I used to know someone who had a very similar set-up. She was quite proud of it. I guess I'm sentimental about them."

Kate frowned. His words sounded right, but he didn't strike her as the type to be sentimental about anything. "I read that they are called putz houses. Is that right?"

"Yes." His attention strayed back to the village. "This one is remarkably similar to Judith's."

Kate stilled. "Judith Delaney?"

"Yes. You knew her?"

"Um, no, but–"

"This is hers, isn't it?"

She nodded before she could stop herself. The man's reaction made her wish she hadn't confirmed the identity.

He clenched his hand into a fist. "I knew it. She lied to me. She told me it was destroyed in a fire. Why would she do that? It doesn't even make sense." He paced, muttering to himself under his breath. He stopped and cleared his throat before moving closer to Kate – so close she fought the urge to take a step back.

Jupiter growled from his spot in the corner, but the old man ignored him. "I must have this set. Remembrances of the good ol' days and all that. How much?"

"Sir, I'm sorry, but I can't sell it to you." Kate hated the waver in her voice, but the man's over-the-top reaction made her wary.

His jaw tightened.

Now she did step back. What was it about this village? She glanced at the houses in the window then back at the man. Jupiter growled again and took a step forward until Kate put her hand up to stop him. "Jup, sit. It's okay." Turning her attention back to the old man, she tried to give her best customer-service smile, but it wobbled on her face. "Sir, you could give me your name and number, and if I decide to sell–"

"I don't have time to wait around, young lady. I'm a very busy man."

"I can see that." She hesitated before deciding it wouldn't hurt to ask. "You were friends with Judith Delaney?"

"That's not the word I'd use," he snapped. "But yes, you could call us friends. We grew up together. I'd always admired this set. It was so well-done. Now that I see it again, I must have it."

He admired the falling-apart cardboard? She looked at his tailored suit and his expensive shoes, his entire manner screaming wealth and privilege. She didn't believe him. He obviously knew something she didn't about these putz houses. Maybe they really were worth more than she had originally assumed. "I'm going to have to think about it, sir."

His smile made her skin crawl. "This isn't the way to do good business, young lady."

"I guess that's my business."

He gave another smirk that sent goosebumps skittering across her arms. "It was just some friendly advice from an old man who has been quite successful over the years."

She took a deep breath. "Did you want to leave your phone number?"

"I'll check back. Don't sell it to anyone else." He headed towards the door. He stopped, his jaw flexing. "Please," he gritted out.

"Yes, sir."

"It couldn't possibly mean as much to you as it does to me."

She raised an eyebrow. She almost responded, but it wasn't

really his business that she was related to Judith Delaney. Besides, even with a blood connection, he was probably right—he definitely would've known her grandmother better than she had.

AFTER A COUPLE HOURS OF RESEARCH, KATE STILL COULDN'T FIND evidence that putz houses had any significant value. The whole set could be worth maybe a hundred dollars. Perhaps the old man who stopped by a couple days ago was simply a collector? Collectors could get very serious and protective about their finds. If that was the case, she could make a very nice profit off the village.

But something didn't sit right. She walked to the window display, Jupiter trailing behind her. The village was actually kind of pretty, nestled into the fake snow and trees she'd placed around it, almost like a child's drawing come to life. But the UPS guy was right—the dark house did look sad among the other decorated buildings. Maybe she should add some decorations to it. It was a Christmas display, after all. She removed it from the window, carefully put it into a small box, and settled it into her backpack. She'd take it home and find some way to make it more festive.

CHAPTER 3

Kate stretched her arms over her head and smiled proudly at the little house on her coffee table. Despite its bedraggled appearance, it had taken her until well after midnight to make a wreath worthy of hanging on its front door. The small bit of red and green added a nice touch of Christmas. She put the house back in her backpack to return it to the shop. Some lights around the roof would be nice, too. Did she have anything that could be used to make Christmas lights? She wandered around her home, looking through drawers and cabinets for something that could approximate lights when the sound of her phone ringing echoed down the hall. Running back to the living room, she grabbed it. "Hello?"

"Is this Ms. Sinclair?"

She didn't recognize the voice but replied in the affirmative.

"Good evening, ma'am."

Ma'am?

"This is Sergeant Fisk with the Sheriff's department. There's been a break-in at your store."

"A what?" Surely she'd heard him wrong.

"A break-in, ma'am." He raised the volume of his tone.

"Yes, I heard you." She rubbed her forehead.

"You did ask..."

"Never mind." Questions swirled inside her head. "What kind of break-in? Is there damage? Did they take anything?"

"There appears to be quite a bit of damage, ma'am. We need you to come down and assess if anything's missing."

"Yes, of course, I'll be right there." She stuffed her phone in her pocket, grabbed her backpack, and ran out the door.

WHEN KATE ARRIVED AT THE STORE, HER HEART PLUMMETED. Hovering in the entrance, she blinked back tears at the destruction. Shards of glass from the shattered front door covered the floor. The store's merchandise lay in heaps, ripped, torn, cracked, and broken. Pottery and vases had been thrown to the floor, pages had been ripped out of books, drawers from furniture lay broken in pieces. Who would do something like this? And why? It seemed like destruction just for the sake of destruction. Was it because she didn't have enough Christmas decorations?

"Ma'am? I'm Sergeant Fisk." The young officer picked his way toward her through the debris.

"Please stop calling me 'ma'am.'"

"Yes, ma'am," he said without humor.

She looked at him from the corner of her eye.

He cleared his throat and looked down at the notebook in his hand. "We have a few questions for you. First, can you tell if anything is missing?"

She shrugged. "It'll take some time to inventory everything, but nothing major is jumping out to me. My most valuable items are still here." Destroyed, but here. "It makes no sense."

The old man and his obsession with the Christmas village came to her mind. She swung toward the front window. The little Christmas village was still there, although each building had been torn apart and lay flat, with fake snow and trees on the ground. Based on how much the old man had seemed to want it, she'd suspect him of stealing it, but not destroying it. Either way, it was certainly worthless now. Kate turned back to the officer. "Do you have any idea who did this?"

"That was actually my next question for you."

She shook her head. "I don't have a clue."

"Do you have any enemies?"

"Not that I know of."

"Have you received any threats?"

"No, nothing. This is a complete shock."

"Can you tell me what time you left the store this evening?" As Kate went through the events of the day with the officer, she wandered the store, searching for something missing, mentally checking off items in her head. An idea flitted into her brain. She stopped and interrupted the officer's suggestion that she install an alarm system.

"It kind of seems like they were looking for something, doesn't it?" She surveyed the wreckage of the shop. "I mean, they opened everything."

Sergeant Fisk scratched his chin. "What would they be looking for?"

"I have no idea."

CHAPTER 4

Alex climbed out of his UPS truck and picked up the two boxes for Out of the Attic, anticipating his interaction with the captivating owner. She seemed to appreciate the pizza yesterday. Maybe today he could build on that success. As he neared the entrance, he slowed, registering the glass on the ground. Inside the shop, Kate sat on the floor, leaning against an antique armoire amidst the broken and destroyed contents of her store. She wiped a tear from her eye, and his chest constricted.

"Are you okay?"

She jumped to her feet, swiping a hand across her face.

He pretended not to notice the tears as he stepped over the threshold. "What happened?"

"There was a spider."

Her attempt at lightheartedness endeared her to him even more. "Did you get it?"

"I think so."

He surveyed the room as if searching for the nonexistent arachnid "But you're not sure?"

She gestured to the mess on the floor. "If it's not dead, it's the only thing left in here that's not."

"You're in here."

"I'm close to dead."

The comment squeezed at his heart. He set the boxes down on some broken glass and took a step toward her. "Seriously though, what happened?"

Kate sighed. "A break-in last night. They trashed the place."

"Kate, I'm so sorry." She looked like she needed a hug, and he really wanted to give her one, but he hung back, unsure of the appropriateness of such a gesture. What if she still thought of him as just the UPS guy? "I'll ask again—are you okay?"

"I'm fine. I wasn't here when it happened."

"That's not what I meant."

"Are you referring to the fact that my entire livelihood is literally smashed to pieces on the floor?"

"I guess so." Heat climbed up the back of his neck. Of course she wasn't okay but he couldn't think of what to say to someone in her situation.

"I'm fine. It's fine."

"So you're not fine."

Her shoulders slumped. "Maybe not. I don't know what to do." She looked at him as if waiting for him to tell her.

"I don't either." He shrugged. "I'm sorry."

She sniffed, seemingly resigned to the fact that no one would know.

"Is it all completely destroyed?" He glanced around again, wincing at the utter destruction. "Maybe some things can be saved. Or salvaged. I mean, that's what you do, right? Fix things up?"

"I don't know. I started to pick through things, but I got so overwhelmed I just sat down and started to..."

When she didn't finish, he guessed the end of that sentence was "cry."

"Is it silly of me to be so upset about this? I mean, it's just stuff. Isn't that what people say? Am I selfish or self-centered to be angry and sad and frustrated and confused and..." A tear rolled down her cheek.

This time, Alex couldn't stop himself from touching her arm. "What? No. Of course not. It's perfectly understandable that you'd be upset. You've worked so hard at this, and it's your career, and..." He trailed off. By her sad expression, his words weren't helping. He tried again. "Of course you're upset. I'm upset and it's not even my stuff. It'd be weird if you weren't upset."

"Thanks."

He shifted, wanting to do more but knowing he had a truckload of packages waiting for him. "I wish I could stay and help, but I have more deliveries."

"I need to call the insurance company anyway."

"If you have a broom, I'll at least sweep up the glass."

"You don't have to do that."

"I'd hate for Jupiter to step in it and–"

"Jupiter! Oh no! He's been in the house since midnight. I've got to go home to let him out." Kate grabbed her keys but stopped awkwardly at the door. "How do I lock up?"

"I don't think you can."

"But what if someone steals something?"

Alex raised an eyebrow at her. Clearly, she wasn't thinking things through this morning.

She threw up her hands in agreement. "Okay, okay, but like you said, there might be some things that can be salvaged. I don't want them disappearing or getting even more ruined than they already are."

"Hold on a minute. I have an idea." Maybe he could help her after all. "Let me call Todd."

"Who's Todd?"

"My brother." Alex pulled out his cell phone and called his

brother, who often spent part of his day across the street at the local coffee shop. Alex explained the situation, got Todd's agreement, and hung up. "My brother is going to come over and watch your store while you go home and take care of Jupiter. And take a nap. And get some food. Everything's worse when you're hungry and tired."

"I can't ask your brother to do that. He doesn't even know me."

"But he knows me, and I'm the one who asked. Don't worry about it. He usually works on his novel over there, but he'll work on it here instead. He's already got his coffee, so he's good to go."

Kate bit her lip, worry evident in her brown eyes. "I don't know if this is a good idea."

"I know you don't know him, but he's perfectly trustworthy. Besides, he couldn't get very far." Alex nodded his head towards the figure coming across the street. The young man had a backpack on his back and a thermos dangling from one of the straps. He had a forearm crutch in each hand and walked haltingly over to the store. Alex leaned over and whispered to Kate, "He was in a car accident. Broke his back. He's doing much better now, though."

Kate watched Todd make his way across the street before turning to Alex. "Thank you." He saw a shimmer of tears in her eyes before she moved around him to stare at the mess of the store. "But he can't watch the shop indefinitely. I still don't know what to do."

Alex hesitated then took the plunge. "How about this: After work I'll pick up some plywood, come back here, and make the door as secure as possible until you can get it fixed."

"I can't ask you to do that."

"Good grief, woman, you didn't ask. I offered."

"Why?"

"Because it's a small town and we help each other out.

Because I enjoy playing the hero. Because I'd like to think we're friends. Is that enough reasons?"

"Yes. Thank you. Again."

"No problem."

Todd arrived at the store and gave a big grin. "Here I am to save the day!"

"Thanks, man. I owe you." Alex clapped him on the shoulder, nearly knocking him over, but Todd didn't seem to mind. "I'll see y'all later." Alex gave a salute and walked back to his truck, whistling a Christmas carol. He hated the circumstances, but it did allow him to spend time with Kate outside of work. And that was a welcome development.

CHAPTER 5

Kate couldn't believe it took a break-in at her store to finally learn the UPS driver's name. His brother called him Alex. She liked it. It suited him. She bit the corner of her lip and shook her head. She was not about to get starry-eyed over her UPS man. Instead, she focused on Todd and their random conversation which ran the gamut from odd to quirky. Deep into the merits of red velvet versus chocolate cake, Kate jumped when Jupiter gave a happy bark and ran to what used to be the store's front door.

Through the broken doorframe, Alex wrestled with several sheets of plywood. And he wasn't alone.

Kate straightened as a small group of people filed into the store.

Alex smiled at her. "I brought a few people I thought might be able to help. This is my sister, Jessie, and my parents, Patrick and Laura Whitlow."

Jessie extended her hand to Kate. "Nice to meet you. Alex mentioned you needed some help sorting things."

"Sorting things?" Kate repeated, dazed by the now-crowded

room. She frowned. Why had he brought them here? And what on earth was she supposed to do with them?

Alex pulled Kate aside with gentle pressure on her arm. "I hope I'm not overstepping. They asked where Todd was, and I told them what happened. They insisted on coming."

"They insisted, huh?"

"Yes we did," Laura interjected herself into the conversation.

Alex smiled. "I told you this is what people in small towns do. I thought while I'm hanging wood, they can help you start organizing things, figure out what's salvageable and what's not."

Kate took a big breath in and slowly let it out. This job seemed impossible but maybe not as impossible as it had before Alex's family had invaded her store. "Um, okay."

"Where should we start?" asked Jessie.

"Um...?"

Concern radiated out of Alex's hazel eyes as he locked gazes with her. "Maybe sort into keep and not keep?"

Kate nodded. Why was her brain not working? Thank goodness Alex was here to give some directions. "Yes, that would be good. And maybe a third pile for things you're not sure about. I can sort through that later."

Todd closed his laptop and stood. "I can help too. Why don't you give us an idea of what you consider fixable before we spread out and get started."

Alex grabbed the plywood and began working on the door while Kate explained what she could repair and what she couldn't. When he finished hanging the wood, he pitched in with the sorting.

The whole family seemed to think they were a troupe of comedians, keeping her entertained throughout the evening with stories and jokes. Jupiter loved it too, walking from person to person, getting tons of pats and back scratches. It was a unique experience for Kate to be around a family who got along so well. She tried to imagine this scenario with her family, but the picture in her mind always ended with arguing and shouting. She thought families like Alex's only existed on TV. Maybe it was an act, more of that southern hospitality thing. Either way, she was grateful for their presence, even if only for the pleasant distraction.

By 10 PM, Kate's back ached, but they had over half the store separated into sections. She rubbed her neck. "I think it's time to call it a night."

No one objected to her statement. They must be as exhausted as she was. As the rest of them gathered their coats, Alex cupped her elbow with his hand to tug her into one of the cleared corners of the room. "I am sorry if I overstepped. I just wanted to help. I thought it'd be a nice surprise, but I think I made you uncomfortable."

"No, it's good." To her surprise, she meant it. "You did help. They helped. A lot."

"Are you sure?"

She put her hand over his, enjoying his touch. "I admit I'm not used to this kind of thing, but it was a nice evening... considering I spent it throwing away half my livelihood." That earned her a quick smile from Alex. Then she tore her gaze from his to stare at the floor. "Um, speaking of apologies, I think I owe you one. For yesterday."

"Yesterday?"

"I kind of overreacted about the dark house. I think I jumped down your throat a bit."

"Did you? I didn't notice."

"Yes, you did. But thank you. And I am sorry."

"If you did, all would have been forgiven already. No worries."

"Thank you." She glanced over her shoulder to see Alex's

family staring at them. She took a small step back from Alex and gave his family a small wave, which they took as an invitation to join them.

"Are you a hugger?" Laura grabbed Kate in a hug without waiting for an answer.

Squished against Laura, Kate managed to squeak, "I don't know?"

"You will be soon if you keep hanging around this family." Todd lightly punched her in the arm. "Although they haven't changed me in 27 years."

Jessie put her arms around Kate for a quick embrace, then pulled Todd into the hug, squeezing him tight. "We'll get him yet." She laughed as he fought to escape, but he chuckled too.

As Patrick gave Kate a hug as well, indecision warred in Alex's eyes. Kate bit her lip to keep from smiling too broadly at his discomfort as she grabbed her bag and Jupiter's leash. "C'mon boy."

Outside in the parking lot, as she watched the taillights of their car pull away, it occurred to her how much she'd missed having people care about her.

Alex stood next to her. "Where's your car? I can walk you to it."

"Oh, I don't have a car." She tightened her grip on Jupiter's leash.

"You don't?" His puzzled expression teased a laugh out of her. "How did you get here?"

"I walked. Like I do every day. It's only about 30 minutes one way."

"You walk an hour to and from work each day?"

She shrugged. "It's good exercise."

He opened his mouth, then closed it before adding, "It's late. Why don't I give you a ride home?"

She nearly refused, but the way her neck and back felt, a ride sounded good. So did getting to a hot bath sooner rather than later. "Okay, thanks. I feel like I've been saying that to you a lot lately."

"Doesn't bother me." He grinned as he loaded Jupiter onto the bench seat of his pickup truck, then held the door as she climbed in.

Once everyone was settled, Alex steered the truck towards the main road. "What did you mean when you said you weren't used to this kind of thing? What kind of thing?"

"Strangers offering to help. Or maybe more accurately, actually accepting their help." She eyed him, deciding she could risk sharing a bit more. "I've been a loner all my life, and I wasn't even trying that hard. People have a tendency to make me nervous."

He braked for a stop sign. "I've seen you with customers. You're great with them."

"That's different. It's just a moment in time, and I'm basically playing a role–helpful sales associate. Being myself, being with a group of strangers, admitting I can't do it on my own... that's all out of my comfort zone."

"Again, I'm sorry."

"Please stop apologizing. It was great of you all to help. I'm normally pretty self-sufficient, but this whole thing left me reeling. Left to myself, I probably would've spent the evening wallowing. Now I feel like progress was made, and I'm ready to keep going tomorrow. Seriously, thank you. Again!" The headlights of a passing car lit Alex's grin in the cab's interior. "You could even say you were almost like a hero."

He laughed. "Almost, huh? I'll take it."

Kate pointed to the next turn Alex should take and they pulled into the driveway of the large Victorian house she still hadn't gotten used to calling home. She opened the door and Jupiter crawled over her to jump out and Kate followed him.

Alex opened his truck door and stood. He whistled, staring at the house. "Nice."

Kate's cheeks grew warm. The house was extravagant for one person and something she never could've afforded on her own. "Thanks. It was my grandmother's."

Surprise registered on Alex's face. "This was Judith Delaney's house. She was your grandmother?"

"You knew her?"

"Knew of her. Everyone in town did. She was like the matriarch of Hemmingway. Never actually met her though. Unless you count running into her one day on a walking trail around Lake Sorren."

"Why wouldn't you count that?"

"Because I literally ran into her. I was nine and playing football with my friends. I was looking behind me and ran smack into her."

Kate coughed to smother a snort. "What did you do?"

"I turned bright red, yelled, 'Sorry,' grabbed the ball, and ran."

Kate laughed.

"But your last name is Sinclair."

"Sinclair is my mother's last name."

"Did you ever visit? I don't think I met you until you moved here last year."

"No."

Kate registered his slightly hurt expression from her short reply but her attention was focused on the house. "Sorry, but there's a light on."

Alex shut his door and joined her on the sidewalk.

"Maybe you accidentally left it on?"

"It's a room I hardly ever go into. And I certainly didn't go in it today."

"You're sure?"

"I'm positive."

"Wait here." He moved to the sidewalk.

She followed him. "I'm not waiting here."

"Will you at least let me go in first?"

"I think I'd prefer that." The break-in had made her more wary than usual and the thought of facing a similar situation on her own made her doubly glad she'd accepted Alex's ride home.

On the front porch, Alex put out his arm to stop her progress. "Was your door damaged like that when you left this afternoon?"

Kate peered at her front door. The wood had splintered and next to the lock, a large gash marred the old wood. Her stomach knotted at evidence of another break-in. "You've got to be kidding me."

He grasped her hand, tugging her back a few steps. "Let's call the Sheriff."

CHAPTER 6

Kate and Alex stood in the middle of her living room, surrounded by emptied drawers, broken furniture, and fingerprint dust. The deputies had just left, and Alex wasn't sure whether he should follow them or not. He knew he wanted to stay, but what did Kate want? She sighed as she sank down onto the couch.

"I can't believe this happened again. And in my home." Jupiter nudged her with his nose. She patted him on the head, then buried her face in his neck. She mumbled something that Alex couldn't hear.

"What?"

She lifted her head. "This confirms it's not random. What do they want?"

"I wish I knew." He sat next to her on the couch. "I'm just glad you weren't home. I wonder if they came during the day, when they knew you were at the store, or if they came tonight, when you'd usually be home." She shivered. Maybe he should've kept that question to himself.

"Do you think they'll come back?"

"I don't know. It seems like they did a pretty thorough job of searching the house already. But who knows if they found what they were looking for?"

"You think they were looking for something specific?"

"Their goal obviously wasn't robbery because they left behind some pretty valuable stuff. And I think if it was random violence, it would've been just the store, or just your house. Not both."

"I thought about that at the store this morning. Things had been opened, like they were looking for something."

"Like what?"

"I have no idea. It's not like I go around hiding–oh!" Her eyes brightened.

"Oh?"

"I don't hide things, but my grandmother did."

"How do you know?"

She reached her hand into the pocket of her jeans. "Because I found this." She withdrew her hand and showed him a key. "I'd forgotten about it."

"Where did you find it?"

"In the dark putz house." She offered the key to him.

Alex took it from her hand. "A key could definitely be relevant. No markings on it. Do you know what it unlocks?"

"No. I was planning on looking around the house to see if there was a locked box or something." She paused. "But I guess someone's already done that."

"But did they find what they were looking for?" He waggled the key in front of her face. "Obviously they didn't find the key."

"How would we know if they found what it unlocks if we don't know what it unlocks?"

"I don't know." He set the key on the coffee table in front of him and observed the destruction around them. "Listen, I don't want to overstep again, but I don't think you should stay here tonight. Or for a while. At least not until the door is fixed."

"I was thinking about that too."

One hurdle conquered. Now for the tricky part. "Why don't you stay with my parents?"

"I couldn't do that."

He had expected the response. "It's kind of your only option."

"No, I'll get a hotel."

"That's what I mean." He waited for her to meet his gaze. "They own the bed-and-breakfast in town. There are no other hotels."

"Seriously?" Her eyes widened, drawing him into their brown depths. A man could get lost in there and not regret it one bit.

"Yep."

"What about Jupiter?"

"He can come too. Just make sure he doesn't chew up my mom's bedspread."

"Hey, he may be a police dog dropout, but he's still a good boy. He only chews his rawhide." She sighed deeply, the sound telling him she'd capitulated. "Fine. Let me go pack some things."

Alex leaned back on the couch. "Wow, that was easier than I expected."

"I'm too tired to argue, especially considering I don't think I'd win in the end." She stood and headed towards the stairs. "I'll be back in a few minutes. Would you mind giving me a ride over there?"

"Of course not. I'll even give them a call and let them know we're coming."

"Like a true hero."

He grinned. He liked hearing her call him that. Now if only he could keep her safe, figure out who did this and why, he could truly be her hero.

CHAPTER 7

The intruder had trashed the bedroom as thoroughly as the rest of the house. Her clothes covered the floor, dumped out of the drawers and ripped off hangers. What was the point? She didn't own anything worth searching for and everything her grandmother owned had been here for years, so why now? Did the key have anything to do with it? Chances were if the key did open a box, whoever broke in had already found it and taken it.

She moved to the closet in search of her duffel bag. Hat boxes, photo boxes, and shoe boxes had been dumped on the floor. She dug through the mess and found the bag under a pile of black-and-white photos. She picked one up and stared at the unfamiliar face looking at the camera. A relative? A friend of the family? She had no idea and had no one left to ask. Someday she'd go through the photos, maybe keep a couple, but post most of them for sale in the shop. She didn't understand why, but a surprising number of people would buy old photos of total strangers. She looked around for the box the photos had been stored in. To sell them, she needed to make sure they didn't get bent and torn. No empty box remained in the closet. Surveying the mess of the room, she spotted a box half-hidden behind the curtains. She grabbed it, but something dropped to her feet as she pulled it from behind the curtain.

She looked down, expecting more pictures, but instead the box had a false bottom which had opened and fallen out, revealing a small, red notebook, barely bigger than the size of her hand. With a lock on it. This couldn't be real. Kate dashed down the stairs, notebook in hand. "I need the key!"

Alex met her in the hallway, key in his hand. "Did you find a box?"

She shook her head as she inserted the key into the lock. It fit. Turning the key, she heard the click of the notebook unlocking.

"No way." She grinned as she glanced at Alex.

"Open it! What does it say?" His excitement fueled her own.

She flipped through the pages. "It's a diary. An old one from the looks of it." She turned back to the first page. "1957. I'm pretty sure that's the year my father was born."

She raised her head, almost knocking it into Alex's chin. When had he gotten so close to her? She took a step back, then had the urge to step forward again, suddenly missing his presence. She shook her head. The shock of the break-ins and finding the locked diary must be getting to her. "But do you think an old diary is what they were looking for? Why would anyone care?"

He shrugged. "Maybe your grandmother tells some secrets."

"Then why not steal it in 1957? Or 1973? Or 2006, for that matter. Literally any other time. Why now?"

"I have no idea. Guess we have to read it."

Kate smiled. "You might be right."

CHAPTER 8

Alex prepared himself for questions as he entered the lobby of his parents' bed and breakfast. His mother raised her eyebrows, hands on hips. "What are you doing here? Are you okay?"

"I'm fine. I thought I'd join y'all for breakfast." By her now-frowning expression, she obviously didn't buy his response.

"Why?"

"You said I had an open invitation to come anytime."

"Yes, but you never do. You don't eat breakfast."

"Maybe I should start. You know they say it's the most important meal of the day?"

His mom tapped a finger on her chin. Alex kept his own expression friendly, hoping she hadn't figured out the real reason for his morning appearance. Then she grinned. "I think I have heard something like that. And you know I love to feed my children. Of course, we always eat breakfast with the guests; I hope that's alright with you." She gestured towards the hallway leading to the dining room, ushering him ahead of her.

"Oh, yeah, that's fine." He headed toward the dining room. "How are your guests?"

"Do you really want to know how they all are, or just one of them in particular?"

Alex turned to his mother. "I feel a bit responsible for her, Ma. I'm the one who brought her here."

"You always were bringing strays to the house." She patted his cheek. "Look, feel responsible, feel protective, feel whatever you want. It's none of my business. But listen," his mom leaned in close and whispered, "she went to grab something from her room, but she's sitting at table two."

Alex bussed his mother's cheek with a kiss. Yep, nothing got past her. "Thanks for minding your own business, Ma." He walked into the dining room and grabbed a plate from the buffet table. He usually woke up at the last minute and downed some coffee for breakfast, but his mother's cooking was too good to pass up. He piled on eggs, a couple of her famous cinnamon rolls, and a few pieces of bacon before pouring a cup of coffee. He met Kate at table two just as she sat back down. "Mind if I join you?"

"Of course not. Have a seat."

He sat, bowed his head for a quick prayer, and dug into a cinnamon roll.

She watched him. "It must be nice to be able to eat like this every morning. Though I guess it's a good thing you have an active job, otherwise you wouldn't be able to keep that slim physique."

He swallowed his bite. "I don't eat here often, actually."

"Oh." A smile played around her lips.

"I mean, I don't usually get up early enough to come over here. I value my sleep."

"Me too. Especially since I went to sleep later than I intended last night. The smell of all this food convinced me it was worth getting up, though."

"Did you have trouble sleeping?"

"I barely tried. I started reading the diary, and it pulled me in." She rested her hand on the book, which lay on the table beside her. "My grandmother was an eloquent writer."

"Any juicy rumors?"

"Not yet. Although reading between the lines, I'd say she was having an affair with someone, but she hasn't named names, so I'm still not sure this is what they were after."

"An affair in the '50s was a pretty big deal, especially for the mayor's wife."

Kate jerked her head up. "She was the mayor's wife?"

"Yeah. You didn't know that?"

She shook her head. "I know very little about her."

"But it was practically part of her name, as in 'Have you met Judith Delaney, the mayor's wife?' 'This is Mrs. Delaney, the mayor's wife.' Sometimes it actually replaced her name, like 'The mayor's wife is coming for tea.'" Alex sat back as Kate studied her plate. How could she be unaware of her grandparents' notoriety and position in town? Even after Judith's husband died and a new mayor was in office, the town had still referred to her as the mayor's wife. Much to the new mayor's consternation.

Kate shifted in her chair. "She wasn't really part of my life."

"But she left her home to you."

"I know. I find it a little strange myself." She took a bite of food and mumbled around it. "Wow, these cinnamon rolls are good."

He caught the not-so-subtle change of subject and decided to go along with it. "My mom's secret recipe."

"Now this is a secret worth breaking in to steal. The diary? Not so much."

He laughed. "I'll tell my mom you said so. She'll get a kick out of that. Speaking of breaking in, I'm off today. Do you need some more help at the shop? Or your house?"

She opened her mouth, but he hurried on before she could say no. "I noticed that you had some shelves broken and a busted table, and things like that. I do some handyman work on the side, so I could help."

Her brow furrowed, but he couldn't tell what was going on in her head. For a couple of minutes, neither said anything while they ate more.

Kate put down her fork. "I hate for you to use a day off like that, but I honestly am a little overwhelmed with the amount of work that needs done. I accept your help, but let me pay you."

He had no intention of taking her money. "We'll talk about payment later." Pleasantly surprised that he'd not had to fight with her about helping, he went back to his cinnamon roll. Six weeks ago—no, six days ago—Alex never would have thought it possible to spend a whole day with Kate. Even with manual labor involved, this was going to be the best day off ever.

CHAPTER 9

Kate read the diary at the counter in her shop while Jupiter snored in the corner. Alex had gone to the hardware store, then would pick up lunch for them. She'd spent the morning sorting through more of the damaged merchandise and chatting with Alex as he did odds and ends around the shop. She could restore things already built, but actual construction was not her forte. She didn't like to admit it, but Alex had skills she needed. It also hadn't escaped her notice that not everything he fixed had been damaged in the break-in. Some things he'd repaired had needed work since she'd signed the lease.

The morning had flown by, despite her worry things would be awkward between them. Even though she and Alex joked back and forth when he delivered packages, they hadn't spent any real time together, and quick wit could only carry a person for so long. Thankfully, her concern had been unfounded, and they had fallen easily into conversation.

She stared out over the partially restored-to-order shop, replaying bits of their earlier conversations it in her mind. It started with Alex asking why she'd become a vintage store owner.

"I've always been interested in refinishing items, fixing broken pieces, turning the old and unloved into new and useful and desirable. I worked in a store similar to this one back in Virginia. The owner took me under her wing, and I learned a lot. But when my grandmother left me a sizeable inheritance—including a home here—I just figured why not give my own store a try."

"Did you always want to be your own boss?"

"I do like the idea, but honestly, the best part of this deal was not having a roommate for the first time in my life."

"Ah, yes, the lone wolf strikes again."

She threw a rag at him. "How about you? Delivering packages seems like it could be fun—get outside, get some exercise..."

"The rain, sleet, and snow takes a little of the fun out of it." He made a face, and Kate didn't think he was entirely joking.

"You don't like the job?"

"It's fine. I don't dislike it."

But Kate sensed something else would have been his first choice. She decided their relationship had progressed enough she could ask. "What was the dream?"

"History professor."

"Really?"

Alex let out a full belly laugh. "Should I be insulted by the surprise in your voice?"

"No!" Kate fiddled with her collar, sure her face flamed scarlet. "That's not what I meant. Just that it's so different from what I've seen you doing—deliveryman, handyman, hero..."

"Well, some professors are heroes too."

"Then why aren't you a professor-slash-hero?

"I dropped out of college when my brother got hurt."

Kate sobered, remembering Todd and how difficult it was for the younger man to move. "Oh, I'm sorry."

He shrugged. "For a while, he needed full-time help. With the B&B, it was too much for my parents, and Jessie had really young kids at the time."

"It was really good of you to change your plans like that." Her admiration for him grew. No one in her family would have done such a thing for her.

"He's family. I didn't think twice. When we were growing up, our age difference kept us from being close, but after all the time we spent together after the accident… he's my best friend now. It was the best decision I ever made."

Kate smiled. The admission definitely put him in the running for that hero label. "Now that Todd's doing better, have you thought about going back to school?"

Alex leaned against a bookshelf he'd finished fixing. "Not really. Maybe a little. I'm pretty happy with the life I'm living right now. But maybe. Someday."

From there they'd rabbit-trailed to places they'd like to travel, their favorite movies, the atrocity of pineapple on pizza, why pockets in women's clothing needed a constitutional amendment, and even tentatively touched on politics a bit. At some point the conversation had changed to hobbies. They both liked reading and hiking. Alex told her about a few of his favorite local hikes and promised to take her on one soon.

Jupiter snorted loudly, breaking Kate's reverie. She tapped her fingers on the diary in her hand. A hike would be nice: beautiful views, some exercise… more time talking with Alex…

Normally that last part would cause some anxiety—she was usually more comfortable being alone and doing things on her own. If she was alone, there was no pressure for her to be who the other person wanted her to be, to make sure she didn't annoy them or anger them. But now, it seemed different with Alex. Relaxed. Easy. Was she actually looking forward to a hike with him? Hoping it would happen sooner than later? She caught herself staring out the window and shook her head. It was time to adjust her train of thought. Flipping to where she'd left off in the diary, she began to read. It only took a few minutes for her heart to start pounding. If what she was reading was true… Oh how she wanted to talk to Alex about this!

CHAPTER 10

Alex arrived with arms full of wood and bags of food. Holding Jupiter back from an exuberant greeting, Kate took the food from Alex and ushered him inside. "You have to hear what I read in the diary."

He chuckled, hefting the wood. "Can I get this put down first? And eat? I'm starving."

She groaned, her eagerness to tell him the secret she'd uncovered making her impatient. "Fine. But be fast."

He stacked the wood against a wall. "This must be good. Grab the plates out of that bag, please." He opened a bucket of chicken and containers of mashed potatoes and green beans. As he filled his plate, he motioned for her to do the same. Then he sat, ready to listen. "Ok, lay it on me. What sixty-year-old gossip did you find out?"

"My father is not the mayor's son."

Alex choked on his chicken. He coughed, reaching for his soda as Kate handed him a napkin.

"You okay?"

He nodded, still coughing a little. "It says that in the diary?"

She pointed to the book lying on the counter. "She says she's pregnant, but she doesn't know how to tell her husband because they've been sleeping in separate bedrooms for over a year, so he'll know the baby isn't his."

"Wow."

"Yeah, I had to know what happened so I started skimming through the diary, looking for entries about the pregnancy. It was an election year, and the mayor didn't want a scandal about his wife cheating on him, so he pretended the baby was his."

"Wow."

"It gets better. Or worse. Or whatever. Depends on how you look at it. But the real father was blackmailing her to keep it a secret."

"I'm overusing the word, but wow."

She pointed her fork at him. "It's an appropriate word. But there's one more thing."

"I'm not sure I can handle any more."

"Just put the chicken down before I tell you. For safety."

He dutifully set the chicken on his plate.

She wiped off her fingers, then spun the diary so he could read the pages as she told him what it said. "She kept evidence of the blackmail. She thought maybe one day she could get even with the father, turn the tables on him, so to speak. Maybe, sometime in the future, it would be important to him to hide the fact that he had an illegitimate son. So she kept proof."

"Your grandmother was quite the forward-thinker. Very conniving."

"Yeah, I'm not sure whether to be impressed or horrified."

Alex leaned back in his chair. "But maybe that's what the thieves were after – the proof."

Kate frowned. "That's what I thought at first, but I keep coming back to the timing. Why now? If the proof's been hidden for over sixty years, why worry about getting it now? Especially since she's dead and can't do anything with it. No one's going to care if a kid was born out of wedlock sixty years ago."

"Good point. But maybe they have some reason we're not considering." He returned to eating his chicken. "Or maybe we're just completely on the wrong track."

"Maybe." She forked green beans into her mouth, chewing as she considered the options. "But how many hidden secrets could one person have?"

CHAPTER 11

The next day, Kate and Jupiter returned to the shop. Kate worked on new display arrangements, trying to showcase the items she'd been able to salvage without making the store appear half empty. Jupiter gnawed on a rawhide. She ignored the knock on the door. Couldn't they see the closed sign?

The person knocked again.

"Kate, it's me."

She recognized Alex's voice and checked her watch: 6:30 in the evening. It was too late for him to be making rounds. And no wonder she was hungry. She unlocked the door and let him in. "Hey there. What's up?"

"I wanted to let you know that I ordered the glass for the front door, and it should be in next week, and then I can finish this up. We should fix the door at your home, too."

"Thank you so much, Alex. You didn't have to do that."

"All part of my handyman services, ma'am."

A shiver of excitement rippled through her at his accompanying wink. "Not that it isn't nice to see you, but you could have called or texted that information."

He cocked his head to one side. "You think it's nice to see me?"

She backpedaled. "Um, well, yeah. It's always nice to see a friend, right?"

His grin told her he'd seen right through her. "Right. But I'm also here to convince you to come to the town Christmas fair tonight."

"Oh, no thank you. That's not really my thing."

"It's Christmas. How can that not be your thing?"

"I don't get wrapped up in the Christmas craziness is all."

His shoulders slumped and disappointment flashed across his face. Kate suddenly wanted to do almost anything to make him smile again. Her stomach growled. "Excuse me, I'm so sorry." She laid her hand on her stomach. "I got caught up in work and haven't eaten since breakfast."

"Perfect!" There was the smile that made her knees weak.

"Excuse me?"

"The fair has some of the best food this side of the Atlantic Ocean. Come with me and I'll buy you dinner."

"I can't let you buy me dinner. I still owe you for all the work you did in here." She didn't think it was possible, but his smile stretched even further across his face.

"Then you can buy me dinner."

KATE TOOK JUPITER OUTSIDE TO DO HIS BUSINESS, THEN PUT HIM in the office with food and water. She gave him a quick scratch behind his ears. "Be good; I won't be gone long. At least you're getting to eat already. I'm jealous."

Despite the cool air, they decided to walk the few blocks to the Christmas fair. Her attempt at a retort to Alex's suggestion for buying dinner failed. She did owe him for all the work he'd done. Besides, she'd suddenly found herself actually wanting to go to the fair. With him.

Alex pointed to a side street. "Let's go this way."

"But that will add another two blocks."

"Five minutes ago you didn't want to go at all, now you're in a hurry to get there? C'mon, this street always has the best Christmas lights in town."

Kate said nothing but followed his lead down the sidewalk. There wasn't an unlit house in sight. Some had colored lights on every roof-line and window; some had deer twinkling with lights or giant Christmas-themed blow-ups in the yard. Many had some version of a nativity scene or Santa's workshop. A few houses stuck with classic white lights, while one or two simply decorated with greenery and candles in the windows.

Alex gestured to the houses. "Isn't it awesome?"

Kate didn't want to tell him the sight of all the bright lights and happy homes depressed her. "If you like this kind of thing."

"You don't?"

"I guess I don't see the point."

"It's Christmas."

"Christmas survived quite well for many years before the invention of Christmas lights."

He walked backwards down the sidewalk in front of her. "I see. Are you a purist? Or maybe you're a Christmas snob?"

"I deserve neither such praise nor such censure."

He halted. "*Pride and Prejudice?*"

Her mouth dropped open. "You knew that?"

"Did I lose a few masculinity points?" He fell into step beside her, his arm brushing against hers.

"Maybe. But it's all right because you gained major literary points. Honestly, I'm rather impressed."

"A lot of my entertainment choices as a child were dictated by my sister. She indoctrinated me young, so by the time I was old enough to realize I wasn't supposed to like chick flicks and classic novels, it was too late. But you're changing the subject. Back to the Christmas lights. Is it that you don't like any lights, or that you prefer an old-fashioned, non-electric Christmas? Like the candles in the windows?"

"I like the candles better than the lights, but it's not about being old-fashioned. It's about all this work for a few weeks of display, then you have to take it all down again. The time, the cost, the energy. And for what?"

"For Christmas." He spread out his arms as if to gather all the lights together in a hug.

"Is that going to be your answer for everything?"

His arms dropped. "Sorry."

They continued silently for a moment before Alex stopped walking again. "Look around. Get out of your head and just look." He turned in a circle, pointing to the houses surrounding them. "It's Christmas. So, yeah, that might be my answer for everything. But Christmas is a pretty good answer. I don't just see strands of electric lights. I see fun, community, family, celebration, memories – old and new. I see love, hope, joy… faith. And that's Christmas."

"I never would've taken you for the sentimental type."

He nudged her with his shoulder. "I'm a total sap. Not ashamed to admit it. When my brother and sister and I were younger, we'd put on our warmest pjs, and my parents would give us our own little thermos of hot chocolate. We'd come into town and walk—or drive if it was really cold—down all the streets and look at the Christmas decorations." He turned to look at the house in front of him and Kate turned too, trying to see it through the eyes of a child.

Alex pointed to a tree that almost disappeared under the amount of lights strung over the branches. "I used to swear the lights were magic. We'd sing Christmas carols and tell stories about past Christmases and laugh and be together." He shrugged. "I know I'm probably romanticizing it. I'm sure us kids bickered and mom and dad were tired and all that, but there was enough—forgive me—Christmas spirit, that I have good memories of it."

Kate gave him a small smile and followed as he walked down to the next house. He directed her attention to a knee-high nativity set in front of a glowing Christmas tree. "There was one house that always had a huge nativity scene out front, like twice the size of this one. Shepherds, wise men, the works. We'd always stop in front of it, and my dad would tell us about the first Christmas, every year. Then he'd quote Luke 2. You know, the speech Linus says in *A Charlie Brown Christmas*?"

Kate nodded. She loved that movie.

"My brother and sister and I would chime in on the words and phrases we knew until eventually one year Dad didn't have to say anything at all. Because we knew every word. And every year after that, the three of us would tell the story and quote the scripture. And every year, when the story was over, everyone would start walking to the next house. Except for me."

Kate turned to face him. The red lights from the tree reflected on his face, illuminating a look of reverence before he glanced at her and smiled.

He focused back on the nativity. "They'd move on, but I'd stand there, slowly turning and looking at all the lights, all the decorations." He spun in a slow circle, taking it all in. "And I'd think, 'They did this for Him.' And I'd..." He swallowed hard. "I'd be in awe, you know, just staring at the lights until someone in my family would come back and drag me to the next house."

As he gazed at her, she bit her lip and turned back towards the house to avoid his eyes.

"You seem like you want to say something."

She shook her head, her emotions tangling together.

"Come on, out with it."

She kept her head down. "I don't want to ruin your memory because it's one of the sweetest things I've heard, and I love it."

Alex tipped her chin up so that their eyes connected. He leaned in, his voice husky. "Tell me. I want to know what you're thinking."

Shivers ran down her spine.

She was thinking now would be a good time for something more romantic than a theological discussion. She blinked and took a step backwards. She gestured to the yard ahead of them. It had a life-sized stormtrooper wearing a Santa hat and holding a candy cane as if it was a gun. "You know that a lot of these people, even some of the Christians, aren't putting up decorations to honor Jesus, right? I don't pretend to understand what their motives are, but I know it's not worship."

"I do know that. But I also know that if Jesus hadn't been born, they wouldn't be putting lights on their houses. They may not understand what they're celebrating, but what better opportunity do we have to explain it? It's like a sneak attack, and they set themselves up for it." He shoved his hands into his pockets. "As I got older, reality intruded a little bit, I won't lie. But walking down this street still makes my heart happy. It's just… it's…"

"Christmas?"

He shoulder-checked her, sending her staggering a bit. "Yeah."

He caught her arm, righting her on the sidewalk as they resumed their walk. "So what's your favorite Christmas memory?"

He wasn't going to let the subject go, was he? "I don't have one."

"What do you mean?"

"I don't have Christmas memories. At least not good ones."

He spun her to face him, halting their walk once more. His eyes held more questions than she could answer in one evening.

She took a deep breath. Was she really going to tell him? She started walking again so she wouldn't have to see pity on his face. "My father and mother had some problems. I don't remember much besides a lot of yelling and screaming. My father left when I was young. He died a few years later. My mother was in and out of rehab, so I spent most of my childhood in a juvenile home. I had some foster homes here and there, but they didn't really work out. Christmas was never a special time for me."

"Kate, I'm so sorry, I had no idea."

She hugged herself. "It happens."

"It shouldn't." They walked in silence for a moment before he asked, "But what about your grandmother?"

"I didn't know she existed until after she'd died."

He sucked in an audible breath.

"My mother said we had no family. Then last year I got a letter from a lawyer saying my grandmother left me her estate. He seemed shocked I wasn't jumping for joy. I didn't know how to tell him I would've preferred to have her in my life when she was alive than to have her money and house when she was dead."

"I have to say, you make so much more sense to me now."

Kate laughed until tears came to her eyes. "Thank you, I think. For the record, I don't hate Christmas. I just prefer to skip all the extra stuff."

"Extra stuff?"

"The only part of Christmas I liked was church. I don't even know who—some Christian group or other—would pile all the kids from the home into a bus and take us to a Christmas Eve service. I guess that's my Christmas memory. The preacher giving the message, everyone singing the carols. I liked that part. I would close my eyes and get lost in the music. It felt real. Everything else seemed like eye-candy, a happy mask people put on for the holidays. Christmas was usually something I wanted to get over with. Problem was that it's a whole season, not just one day. The decorations came out earlier and earlier, and I didn't want to see them. I felt like the real world and the Christmas world were two separate things, and the Christmas world—the so-called Christmas spirit—was an act, a farce. That's not what they were like, what the world was like, the other eleven months of the year. So I wanted no part of it. But I still go back to that little baby in the manger and what He grew up to be. That's the part I believe."

Alex slung an arm around her shoulders. "That's the important part."

CHAPTER 12

At the Christmas fair, they made a beeline for the food tents. Kate's stomach had made several loud demands and while the gurglings made her blush, Alex thought it was kind of cute. He tried to pay for the meal, but Kate got her money out faster.

"Fine," he said, "but I'm buying the hot chocolate."

"Deal."

Alex loved the sparkle in her eyes when she felt like she won.

They'd found a place to sit when the sound of a trumpet warming up echoed through the night. Alex looked at his watch. "I didn't realize how long it took us to get here. Grab the food." He gathered the cups of hot chocolate as Kate stacked two Styrofoam cartons and followed him.

"Where are we going?"

"To the one part of the fair I know you're going to like." They walked to the other side of the fairgrounds and found seats on a curb facing an old-fashioned gazebo. "Just in time." At that moment, a brass ensemble started playing a rousing rendition of "Hark, the Herald Angels Sing."

A smile formed on her face, and she watched for a moment

before grabbing a meat pie from the box of food balanced on her knees. She took a big bite and moaned with happiness. "Good call."

"The band or the pie?"

She glanced at the ensemble, then at her food. "Both."

Alex waved his own meat pie in the direction of the musicians. "Recognize anyone?"

Kate scrunched up her nose as she leaned forward. "Is that your dad on trumpet?"

"Yep, and Jessie's over there on the French horn."

"That's so fun! I didn't know they played."

"The fair has Christmas concerts every other night. Tonight there's also a choir and some soloists. Mom and Todd are in the choir."

"A musical family. What about you?"

"I play drums. The concert on Wednesday will have a band performance, and I'll be playing then."

"I'm impressed."

"You haven't heard me yet."

"This is true." She returned her attention to the meat pie.

Alex alternated between watching his family and watching Kate. She would get lost in the music, eyes closed, swaying along. Singing softly when the choir did their sing-along. It was the most content he'd ever seen her. If it were up to him, he would give her evenings like this a lot more often.

CHAPTER 13

After the fair, they walked back to Kate's shop. Alex waited by the door as Kate released Jupiter from the office. He ran to her, then darted over to Alex, then back to Kate, his tail wagging so hard his butt shook. Kate burst into laughter.

"You saw us a few hours ago, Jup. It's not like we're returning from war."

Alex knelt as Jupiter made his way back to him. He rubbed the dog's face but kept his focus on Kate. "You going to the B&B? Let me drive you."

"Actually, I need to go home first. I need to grab more food for Jupiter."

"No problem. I'll drive you there first."

"I'm fine. I walk all the time."

"Yes, I know, but it's dark and it's cold. Please let me drive you."

She considered for a moment then nodded, and he ran to the truck and opened the door, motioning for Jupiter to get in. He waited by the open truck door as she locked the store before climbing into his truck.

"Is it really that hard letting people help you?"

"I'm used to doing things on my own." But she could get used to a certain UPS driver's assistance.

"Some of us like to help."

"I've noticed." Alex cranked up the heat. The temperature had dropped while they were at the fair.

They'd barely left the lights of town when Kate heard something behind them. "Do you hear that?" She craned her neck to look. "I don't see any cars on the road, but it sounds like an engine."

Alex glanced in the rearview mirror. "There are no headlights behind us, but it does sound like a vehicle."

"And it's coming fast." The words barely left her mouth when the truck jerked forward with a crunch of metal.

Kate flung one hand in front of Jupiter and used the other to brace herself against the dashboard. Jupiter whined, trying to crawl onto Kate's lap. Kate wrapped her arms around him. "It's okay, boy." But it wasn't okay. "Did someone just hit us?"

Alex tightened his grip on the steering wheel, his knuckles white, and didn't answer. The other vehicle slammed into the truck again, pushing it forward with a screech of metal. Fighting to keep the truck under control, he slammed on the gas and shot forward. Kate whispered a prayer for their safety.

Wrenching the wheel, Alex did a quick U-turn in the middle of the road to face the other way. His headlights caught the car racing towards them. Alex jerked the wheel, drove off the road, and hit the brakes.

Kate tried to catch her breath as the other car flew past. Only when the sound of the engine faded away did she feel she could draw air properly into her lungs.

Alex clicked on the overhead light. His hands ran up her arms. "Are you hurt?"

She mentally ran through a checklist of her arms and legs and everything in between. "No. Are you?"

"I'm fine." His jawline firmed. "But that was on purpose."

She sucked in air as the realization dawned on her. Someone had tried to ram them off the road. Or worse.

Alex called the Sheriff's office. When he hung up, he took her hand and squeezed it.

She squeezed back. "Was that because of me?"

"I don't know."

"They trash my store, then my house. Now this." Tears trembled on the edges of her lashes. Alex could have been hurt because of her. "I'm so sorry."

"What are you apologizing for?"

"It's my fault. I'm obviously being targeted, although I don't know why. You could've been hurt. You could have been killed! Your truck has to be damaged. If I hadn't been in your truck—

"Are you kidding me?" He put his hand on her cheek, stopping the flow of words. "Thank God you were in my truck. Do you know what that car would've done if you'd been on foot?"

Red and blue flashing lights shone through the windshield as a Sheriff's car pulled up in front of them. Kate pulled her gaze away from Alex's as Sergeant Fisk got out of his car. She gave a small sigh and opened the door.

As they explained what happened to the sergeant, Alex tensed at the sound of something coming from the opposite direction. He peered into the darkness. He could hear the vehicle loud and clear, but he saw no headlights. His heart thumping hard, he shoved Kate to the side of the road. The car slowed, presumably at the sight of law enforcement. Its headlights flashed on, and the vehicle drove past them at a normal speed. Anger churned in Alex's gut, and he sprinted after the car, running a hundred yards before realizing he couldn't catch it. Jogging back, he yelled out to the officer, "That was the same car that rammed us."

"How do you know?"

"Same headlights and grill pattern." Frustration made his blood run hot. They lost their chance to find out who had gone after them tonight. "The hood and bumper were damaged, and the first three letters of the plate were YMP."

"But why would they come back?" Kate's question rang in the cold night air.

Sergeant Fisk's grim face told Alex the officer had reached the same conclusion he had.

"I reckon to finish the job, ma'am."

CHAPTER 14

Kate lay in bed, wide awake, absentmindedly running her hand across Jupiter's back as he lay curled up beside her. She'd had a long but fruitless argument with the Whitlow family about whether she should continue to stay at the B&B. If she was being targeted, she didn't want to bring danger to their home and guests. In the end, they'd convinced her she'd be safer at the B&B. Even still, Alex was sleeping on the sofa in the den. They had a room for him, but he wanted to stay close to the front door.

When had he become her designated protector?

She kept circling back to why anyone would want her dead. Kate's thoughts raced as fast as her heart pounded every time she thought of what happened in the truck. Restless and scared, she only knew one thing to do. She tossed the blankets off and swung her legs over the side of the bed. Resting her elbows on her knees, she buried her face in her hands. "Lord, I don't know what's going on, and, worse, I don't know what to do. I'm confused and scared, Lord. I need your peace, and I wouldn't mind a little wisdom too."

She continued to pray—for the safety of the Whitlows and

their guests, for her to be able to rebuild her store and career, for resolution to this strange situation. When a brown-haired, green-eyed, grinning face came to mind, she prayed for Alex as well. She'd never had someone who cared enough to camp out on a sofa. After being alone for so many years, it felt strange to have people concerned about her wellbeing. Strange… but nice.

She prayed until her eyes grew heavy, then she finally crawled back under the blanket and fell asleep.

THE REST OF THE WEEK PASSED WITHOUT INCIDENT. THE STORE remained closed, and Kate spent her time fixing broken antiques, documenting destroyed items, dealing with the insurance company, walking Jasper, having breakfast with Alex at the B&B, watching his band play at the fair, and sharing dinner with him and his family in their home next to the B&B.

It was weird to be eating with other people, since she'd nearly always eaten alone, but her love for his family grew with each meal. Their funny ways and kindness soothed her nerves. And Alex was becoming an early riser. Kate looked forward to their breakfasts, but she didn't want to dwell on why. This family thing was temporary, and soon enough, she'd go back to being on her own. Which is what she wanted. It was familiar, comfortable, and safe.

ON SATURDAY MORNING, WHEN KATE ARRIVED DOWNSTAIRS, ALEX was at their table, almost finished with his plate of pancakes and bacon. He saluted her with his coffee mug. "Hey, there."

She eyed his plate. "Hungry?"

"Not anymore." He grinned. "I thought today we could get a new door for your house. And maybe an alarm system?"

"Jupiter is my alarm system."

"Jup is great, no offense to him, but he is a police dog dropout for a reason."

"He was too sweet and friendly!" Kate huffed in her dog's defense since he was still in the bedroom and couldn't defend himself. "That's not a bad thing."

"In most cases, not at all, but he won't be much help during a break-in." Alex shook his head. "At least promise me you'll think about an alarm system?"

"Sure." Thinking didn't mean doing.

"Good. But either way, the door needs to be fixed before you can stay there again. I happen to be available today. Interested?"

Kate nodded, hiding a grin at the thought of spending the day with Alex.

"If you get a breakfast biscuit or a cinnamon roll, you can take it with us and eat in the truck."

"Are you in a hurry?"

Red crept up Alex's neck to infuse his face. "No, I'm sorry. I just tend to go a hundred miles an hour when I've got a plan. You can eat whatever you want. And please, take your time."

She allowed the smile to spread across her face at his admission. "It so happens that a breakfast biscuit sounds pretty good. We can leave now."

He jumped up from his chair. "I'll be at the truck. Meet you there." He gathered his trash and left. Kate smothered a laugh and headed toward the breakfast bar. When she arrived at his truck, biscuit and cinnamon roll in hand, she found him talking with Sergeant Fisk.

"Ms. Sinclair, I was just coming to speak with you. We found a car abandoned in a landfill outside of town. It has front-end damage and paint chips that appear to match Alex's truck, so we're fairly certain it's the vehicle that hit y'all. A cursory glance shows it's spotlessly clean on the inside, so I doubt we'll get any prints. Plus, it's been reported stolen."

Kate sighed. Even progress left them standing still. "Thank you, Sergeant."

"I'll let you know if forensics turns up anything, but it will be a while."

As he walked back to his cruiser, Alex squeezed Kate's shoulder. "I'm sorry it wasn't better news."

She shrugged. At this point, she wasn't holding out much hope the crimes would ever be solved. "Let's just get my door fixed."

"There's a store a few towns over I thought we might check out. It's like a combination antique store and hardware store. I called ahead with the dimensions, and they have some doors in stock."

CHAPTER 15

They wandered around the store, and Kate made a mental note to come back here after she got her insurance check – there were several furniture pieces she could restore and sell in her own shop – but she wasn't enjoying it as much as she normally would. Ever since talking to Sergeant Fisk, frustration had her on edge. They hadn't made any progress in figuring out who was targeting her, and she was so done with looking over her shoulder, worrying about her new friends, and wondering about all the whys and whats. She needed resolution. She wanted to go back to normal. She jumped as Alex laid a hand on her arm.

"The owner said he's got a stack of old doors out back. Ready to go have a look?"

She followed him through the maze of overflowing shelves to where the owner had stacked flat pieces like doors outside under a covered porch. Several doors could work for her home. After a few moments of indecision, she selected an old cross and Bible door that still had its hinges. It needed some character added to bring it back to life, so she also bought green paint, along with the wood Alex needed to fix the door frame. They put it all in the back of the truck and climbed into the cab.

Alex grinned. "That was fun. When you come back to buy more stuff, can I come with you?"

Without warning, confusion and wariness washed over Kate. She didn't understand the kindness radiating from this good-looking man sitting beside her. In her experience, no one acted like this without an ulterior motive. "Why are you doing all this?"

"What do you mean?"

"Fixing things for me, giving up your days off, sleeping downstairs on a sofa… why?"

"I told you, we're a small town. We help our friends."

She crossed her arms in front of her. "I think it's more than that." The words rushed out, filling the cab. "I think it's a duty for you, like something you have to do."

"What?" Alex flicked the turn signal. "Kate, I want to help you. Honestly, the real reason…. I like you and I… I just want to help."

"And I appreciate it. But… I guess it's…" She fumbled for the right words. "Driven. You seem so driven."

"You say it as if it's a bad thing."

"It is if it that's the real reason you help people. If it's like a compulsion." There, she'd said what needed to be said.

He stared at her, his eyebrows raised. "Are you questioning my motivation?"

The truck drifted towards the verge. Kate grabbed the bar above her head and pointed towards the ditch running alongside the road. Alex jerked the wheel to put the truck back in the lane and stared out the windshield.

Silence built in the car. She knew she'd crossed a line, pushed too far, and upset Alex. He gripped the steering wheel hard, his knuckles white. But still, something drove her to poke the bear.

She shifted in her seat to see him better. "I just think—

Alex held up a hand to stop her. "I like helping people, okay? And I'm good at it. There's nothing more to it."

"I think it's that hero thing you once mentioned."

"That was a joke."

"Maybe not as much as you'd like to think. You have a savior complex or something. It could be control issues, but I think it's more than that. You really do want people to look at you as their hero."

"You're making a lot of assumptions based on one incident."

"It's not just one incident." Kate warmed to her subject. "It's at least three with me alone. Not to mention that you seem to be on a first-name basis with every hardware store owner in a fifty-mile radius, leading me to assume you've done this before. And then there's your brother."

A warning marched across his face. "What about my brother?"

"You dropped out of school, gave up your dreams, everything to help him."

"Of course I did. He's my brother. He's family. Look, I'm very sorry that you don't know what that's like—no kid should grow up without a loving family—but it's what we do. Same with small town communities—we help people, we put others first, we're not selfish. They'd do the same for me if the situation called for it."

Kate shifted to stare out the window. What was wrong with her? Why was she picking a fight? She wasn't used to someone being nice to her without expecting something in return, but that didn't mean there weren't good people out there. The truck stopped in front of her home and Alex climbed out without a word. She watched him through the back window as he untied the rope holding the door in the bed of the truck. Making her way to the back, she grappled with another knot.

"I'm sorry. I was blunt and I went too far."

He stopped working the rope. His gaze locked on her.

She sighed. "I like figuring people out, finding out what makes them tick. Call it a defense mechanism, but if I know what to expect from people, then I don't get surprised or hurt by them."

Alex leaned against the truck. "That's a tough way to go through life."

"It's all I know." She swallowed hard, forcing the words out. "You're right. I don't know what family is like."

"I shouldn't have said that."

"No, you were right. I judge everything—and everyone—based on my own experiences, but you've had different experiences, so… I was wrong to do that." She cleared her throat. This was the part she hated. "Forgive me?"

"No worries, Kate. We're good." His immediate response loosened the knot in her stomach, but she stared at the ground, still embarrassed by her behavior.

With a calloused finger he lifted her chin, then ducked his head to meet her lowered gaze. "I mean, if you're okay with that." His lips twitched and mischief sparkled in his eyes.

She bit back a smile and pretended to think. "Does it mean you'll still help me hang my new door?"

"Well, now it might cost you."

"Oh really? What's it going to take?"

Alex took a step closer and ran his hand down her arm, grasping her fingers in his. He bent his head low, and Kate held her breath. What kind of payment did he have in mind? Her eyes strayed to his mouth.

"Have dinner with my family tonight."

She let out her breath on a quick laugh. "I've had dinner with you and your parents every night this week."

"This would include my sister and her family too. And…" He mumbled something she didn't catch.

"What?"

"And we're going to decorate the Christmas tree."

"Oh." She pulled her hand from his, all thoughts of payments fleeing. "I don't think so."

"Come on, it's just a tree. You might even have fun."

"It's not that. Or it's not only that. It's a family thing. I can't intrude."

"You wouldn't be intruding. I invited you."

"But the rest of your family didn't."

"They wouldn't mind."

Kate considered it for a moment. Decorating for Christmas was something she didn't do. Then add in his family, and it sounded way too personal and intimate. "I'm sorry, Alex, I don't think I'd feel comfortable with that."

He studied at her for a moment, then wrestled the door from the back of the truck. "It's ok, I get it. I'll think of some other way you can pay me back." He raised his eyebrows and gave her a grin that made her heart race before he carried the door up the sidewalk.

Kate watched him walk away then pulled the pieces of wood from the back of the truck. "Alright then." She followed him to the house, a slow smile on her lips.

CHAPTER 16

As Alex fixed the door, along with a few other necessary repairs throughout the house, Kate rolled up her sleeves and cleaned. Since the house was bigger than the store, it would take more time to get it all done. She also packed more clothes to take with her to the B&B. Passing the open closet with the photos still spilled on the floor, she decided to box them up to take with her as well. Maybe she'd have some time to sort through them. By the time five o'clock rolled around, her body ached, a new front door hung in the place of the broken one, and her stomach growled its need of food. When they arrived at the B&B, Todd stood outside talking with Jessie and another man while two kids ran in circles around them. Jessie enveloped Kate in a hug as soon as she exited the truck. "Come meet my family."

Alex swung the boy over his head as Jessie and Kate reached the group.

"Kate, this is my husband, Cameron, and our twins, Harriet and Harry."

"Mom!" The girl stamped her foot while rolling her eyes in the classic gesture of exasperated kids everywhere.

Harriet and Harry? Who would do that to their children? Was it a twin thing? Kate pasted a polite smile on her face. "Nice to meet you all."

Cameron shook her hand. "I see you haven't learned to say 'y'all.' But nice to meet you too."

"Mom, tell her our real names!" The girl's voice held a note of desperation and whine.

"What?" Kate frowned as she swiveled to look at Jessie and apparently not Harriet.

Jessie's eyes danced with amusement. "I'm sorry. I always say that so I can watch people's reactions, but ever since they turned six, they're not playing along very well. These are my honest-to-a-fault, beautiful children, Audrey and Cameron Jr. We call him J.R."

Audrey huffed, then dashed off to attack Alex along with J.R.

"By the way," Jessie added, "your reaction was perfect—your eyes merely went super big. Are you here for dinner and decorating? I assume my brother was smart enough to invite you?"

Kate shot Alex a look, but he ignored her, keeping his attention on the twins. She bit her lip. "I really don't want to barge in on family time."

Jessie waved her hand. "Oh, don't be ridiculous. You'd be doing no such thing."

"No, really—"

The screech of the screen door interrupted her as Laura came out of the house. "Why are y'all standing outside in the cold? Get in here. Kate, you're joining us, right?"

"We're trying to convince her, Ma. That's why we're still outside," Alex yelled while hoisting J.R. over his shoulder.

"I don't want to intrude." Kate's protest sounded weak, her resolve crumbling in the face of such warmth.

"Nonsense. I already have a place set for you. You're part of the family now." Laura stepped back into the house, effectively ending the conversation and calling everyone inside.

Kate lingered beside Alex, as the twins ran ahead, pulling their parents along. "Did you put them up to this?"

"Nope, but I told you you'd be welcome." He swept his hand in front of him, indicating for her to go first through the door. "As she said, you're family now. Like it or not."

CHAPTER 17

Her stomach full, Kate helped to load the dishwasher. "Everything was delicious, Laura. As usual. Thank you so much for including me."

"It's our pleasure, dear."

"Not just for tonight. You've fed me all week, and it's the best I've ever eaten."

"First of all, we love having you. Second, you bring Alex around, and a mother will never complain about her son visiting more often."

"I bring…? He doesn't always eat here?"

"No, dear. He has his own life. He comes over several times a month and, of course for special family get-togethers, but certainly not every night for a week. Not until you were here." She winked.

Kate stood there with a dish in her hand until Laura took it from her and put it in the dishwasher. "There. Time for the tree. You're going to help, right?"

"Oh, um…" Her pulse skittered at the thought of participating in the holiday tradition.

"It's the least you can do after we've fed you all week." Laura winked again and left the kitchen. Kate stood speechless for a moment, realizing she'd set herself up for that. Nothing to it but to hang a few ornaments, then escape to her room. When she entered the living room, a large, fresh, pine tree stood centered in front of the bay window. Boxes of lights and ornaments covered the floor and coffee table. Alex squatted down next to a pair of legs sticking out from under the tree.

"Ah, good, y'all are finally joining us." Alex's father's voice came from underneath the greenery. "Alex and I are almost done with the lights, and then the fun can begin."

"No one else is allowed to help with the lights," said Jessie. "They're very serious about it."

Alex's father shimmied out from under the tree. "Not true. Anyone can help if they're willing to do it right, but y'all just want it done fast."

"There's a right way?" Kate assumed it didn't matter as long as the lights were strung around the tree.

"Yes," answered Alex.

"No," chimed in Jessie. "But there is their way. Which they are convinced is right."

"Some people just put lights through the branches. We do that, too, but first we wrap the trunk with lights." Patrick placed his hands on his hips as he surveyed his handiwork. "It's a bit difficult and scratchy, but it makes the tree glow from within."

Jessie shrugged. "I can't argue that it looks nice when they're done."

"Which they finally are. Bring on the ornaments!" Todd called. The rest of the family reached for boxes and ornaments. Kate watched, mesmerized by their choreography, the back and forth to the tree. Alex pressed an ornament into her hand.

She didn't take it from him. "I don't know what to do. I don't want to mess it up."

"You've never decorated a tree?"

She shook her head.

"Okay." He gently closed her fingers around the decoration. "Every ornament has a loop of string or a hook. Pick a branch and hang it up. You can't really make a mistake."

The ornament in her hand was made of clay and obviously painted by a child, but she couldn't quite tell what it was. "This is... interesting."

"I made it when I was five. It's supposed to be an elf."

"Um, yeah, I can see that." But she couldn't, not really.

He snorted softly. "Liar. But thank you. Now go hang it up."

"If you made it, don't you want to hang it up?"

"There's plenty of others I made. Go on." He put his hand on her back and gave her a gentle push.

As she got closer to the tree, she noticed none of the ornaments were the colored balls or coordinating snowflakes and the like that she'd always seen during the season. Some ornaments were store-bought and some homemade, but there was no pattern, no color theme, no matching. "I like these ornaments."

"Thank you, dear," Laura said. "We go with a red-and-white theme at the B&B, but here at home, all our ornaments have meaning to us in some way. It's truly a family Christmas tree."

"I love that idea."

"Good, now hang up that ornament or we'll never get done." Patrick gave Kate another little push towards the tree.

"Dad!" Jessie chided. "Take your time, Kate."

Kate found a spot that looked right to her and hung the ugly elf on a branch. She stood back to gauge its location amidst the others. Her very first ornament.

"No time for lolly-gagging and admirin', Kate-girl. Go get another one."

"Dad!" Jessie rolled her eyes. "Good grief, it's not a timed-event."

"But the hot chocolate comes next!"

Jessie nudged Kate with her shoulder. "In his defense, it is good hot chocolate."

"I'm all for good hot chocolate," Kate agreed and set to work.

A couple hours later, every branch of the tree sagged under the weight of ornaments, leaving Kate to worry it wouldn't make it through the night. Laura dropped onto the couch with Audrey as Jessie put a lid on the last empty box. Todd and J.R. played some horrible racket on the piano, while the rest of the men went to get hot chocolate and snacks from the kitchen. Kate walked slowly around the tree, studying each ornament. She reached out and gently touched one, turning it to face the right direction.

Jessie came up beside her and threw an arm over her shoulder. "Thank you. That was the most fun we've had decorating the tree in a long time."

"I agree," said Laura. "It's always my favorite thing to do at Christmas, but telling you the stories of each ornament—reminiscing about previous Christmases—it really made this time special."

"Almost worth all the extra time it took." Patrick came into the living room with a tray of mugs and a grin. So that's where Alex got his smile.

Alex followed, carrying yet another box. "You gotta help me with this, Kate. It's the most important part." He set it on the table and pulled out bubble-wrapped pieces, setting them next to the box. Then he unwrapped each piece, revealing a gorgeous, hand-painted nativity set.

Kate picked up a shepherd. "It's beautiful. Do you put it on the mantle?"

"Nope, we put it on the floor."

"What? No, you..." The reaction burst from her in horror at the careless treatment of such a meaningful part of Christmas, but she stopped herself, having no right to trample on their traditions.

"We put it under the tree."

Kate paused a moment. "Why?"

Laura answered. "It's the best gift. Eventually, there will be other presents under the tree, so we like to make sure this one's placed first, front and center. It's a reminder of why we're celebrating. And it reminds us that our gift-giving is to commemorate the greatest gift ever given."

Put like that, Kate could see that the shepherds, wise men, angels, and Christ family had a place of honor. She sent a quick side eye to Alex, knowing he'd intentionally set her up. He dipped his head, intently arranging the fabric laid out under the tree, but Kate could see the corner of his mouth quirked up. She rolled her eyes as she moved to join him under the tree. Together, they reverently set up the nativity. Then he handed her a star with a hook. "The last ornament," he said. "Hang it right above the stable." She did as instructed, then sat back to gaze at the scene they'd created. She cleared her throat and blinked quickly, surprised to find herself a little choked up.

Alex lifted a hand and gently wiped a tear off her cheek. "Good job," he whispered. "You're redeeming the Christmas traditions, one at a time."

His words washed over her, loosening another brick in the wall she'd built around her heart, and she couldn't help but smile.

J.R. raced into the room holding a box. "Look, grandma, we forgot a box."

"I don't recognize that one, sweetie."

"It was by the front door." J.R. thrust the box out towards Laura.

"Oh, that's mine," said Kate, recognizing it. "It has a bunch of my grandmother's old photos. I was going to sort through them this evening in my room."

Laura accepted the box from her grandson. "I love old

pictures. It's so much fun to look at the old styles—the classic cars, the crazy hair." She held up the box. "May I?"

"Of course." Kate settled in beside her on the sofa, delighted to have company to go through the photos. She felt content, warm, happy. She'd never known being part a family could fill so many of the empty spaces in her heart. This Christmas was opening her eyes in more ways than one.

CHAPTER 18

Alex sat on the floor by the coffee table, half-listening as his mom told stories about some of the people she recognized in Kate's old photographs. He loved how his family had embraced Kate. They hadn't blinked an eye at her being part of the evening's Christmas tradition. As he watched them interact with each other—laughing, teasing, talking—it felt like she was always meant to be a part of them.

A photo Jessie tossed onto the table slid sideways, and Alex caught it before it hit the floor. The photo showed a serious-looking man and a young Judith Delaney standing in the middle of a living room. He blinked, then focused on the composition of the photo, excitement building. "Kate, look at this."

She tossed a glance at the photo he held out to her. "I already saw that one."

"No, you need to take a closer look." He pointed to the bookcase behind Judith.

Kate narrowed her eyes as she studied the photo, then grabbed the picture from his hand. "Oh my word! It's the dark house."

"The dark house?" Laura asked.

Kate pointed to the small cardboard house in the picture. "It's part of a Christmas village my grandmother had, but this one didn't have any decorations on it, so Alex called it the dark house."

"But look at her clothes and the trees outside the window," Alex prompted. "It's clearly spring or summer, not Christmas-time. Yet the dark house is still on display."

"So maybe it's not a dark house after all. Maybe it's just not a Christmas house."

"You found the key in one of the other houses." Alex knew he was onto something. "Maybe the proof of their affair was kept in another. And now that I think about it, the dark house was not at your store after the break-in. That must have been what they were after."

Jessie's eyebrows drew together. "But if they got what they wanted, why would they break into her house later?"

"Because they didn't find the dark house at the store," Kate answered. "I have it."

"What do you mean?"

"I thought I might try to decorate it, so I took it home. It wasn't in the shop during the break-in. But when I finished decorating it, I put it in my backpack to take back to the shop, and it's been in my bag ever since."

"The backpack you've been carrying around with you all week?" Alex rose to his feet. Most of his family members wore puzzled expressions but not Kate. She met his gaze, her face telling him she'd come to the same conclusion as he had.

"That's the one."

Kate dashed for the bag sitting next to the door. She pulled out a cardboard box, brought it back to the sofa, and gently removed the dark house.

"Nice wreath," Alex said, his heart warming at how far she'd come to embrace the Christmas season.

Kate gave a shy smile. "Thank you. I was even thinking of adding some lights."

Alex put his hand over his heart. "No, not the dreaded electric lights."

"Well, it was supposed to be a Christmas decoration. Or so I thought." She turned the house around in her hands. "It's sealed closed."

"How did you open the other one?" He eyed the house as she rotated it.

"I dropped it and the roof came off."

"Rather than dropping this one, let's use my pocket knife." He handed her the knife, and she carefully cut along the seam between the walls and roof. The roof popped off and a stack of folded papers fell out of the house.

"Oh, wow," she breathed. She unfolded the top piece of paper and scanned it. "It's a love letter. A juicy one." She flipped the page over. "It's unsigned."

She handed the first letter to Alex, who skimmed the contents while she worked her way through the other papers. She unfolded one and gasped. "This isn't a love letter. It's blackmail. It talks about the baby. It says if she wants him to keep quiet about the fact that it's his, then she's got to pay him. Also unsigned, of course."

"Maybe the next letter tells you more." Alex stacked the papers.

She bent her head over another page. "It says in lieu of monthly payments, he will accept 500 acres of land owned by the Delaneys."

"Wow." Jessie sank back onto the couch. "This is so scandalous. I love it."

Alex rifled through letters, double-checking for a name. "These are all unsigned. It's evidence, but of who?"

Kate shrugged. "I don't know."

"Your grandmother said she had proof. Keep looking."

Kate unfolded more letters without coming across a name. Finally, only two pieces of paper remained. She unfolded the first one and silently read.

"This is it! It's a copy of a deed!" She quickly scanned the document. "For 500 acres... it's the same handwriting as the letters."

"By who?"

"A deed from who?"

"Who's it to?"

Alex ignored the questions chorusing around from his family and kept his eyes on Kate.

"It's from my grandparents." She squinted at the page. "And it's selling the land to James Lacey."

"Oh. My. Word." His mother's face wore the same shocked look he was sure his did.

"Who is James Lacey?" Kate furrowed her brow.

"He's like the richest man in North Carolina," his mother said. "He owns a massive luxury resort–

"Probably on about 500 acres," Alex mumbled.

Laura narrowed her eyes at him for interrupting, then continued. "A resort, complete with casinos, which is where a lot of his money comes from. He also owns a couple shopping malls and several warehouses, although no one knows what he does with those."

"There are plenty of rumors about what he does with them, and it's nothing good," Patrick added.

"And he scares everyone." Jessie hugged a pillow to herself.

"He's a mean old man." His mom picked up the photo Alex had found. "And this is him."

Kate studied the picture. He looked familiar. She tried to imagine him older. "This might be the guy who came into my store asking about the village."

Jessie leaned forward. "Dapper guy in a gorgeous suit, with neat white hair and a cane he doesn't need?"

"Yes!"

"That's him."

Alex had heard enough to know the man must be behind the attacks, although the why wasn't completely clear yet. "I think it's time to call the Sergeant Fisk."

"Wait." Kate grabbed his hand. "There's one more piece of paper from the house." She held it up as the room grew quiet.

"What does it say?" Jessie bounced in her seat.

Kate stared at the paper. "It's says it's a Transfer on Death Deed. What on earth is that?"

Patrick took the deed from her. "It means that when the current owner dies, the property is automatically given to whoever's named in the deed. No need for a will or probate or anything like that." He put on a pair of reading glasses. "This is strange. It's dated about ten years after the first deed, but it's for the same 500 acres."

Alex had an uncomfortable feeling this might explain why someone had been targeting Kate. His father continued, "It's from James Lacey to Judith Delaney." He kept reading. "This is interesting: it states that if she's already passed by then, then the property goes to her heirs."

Jessie squealed, "Kate, that's you."

Alex put his hand on Kate's shoulder. He took a breath before speaking. "And it's motive for someone to want you out of the picture."

CHAPTER 19

The next morning, Sergeant Fisk stopped by the shop with an update.

"We talked with Mr. Lacey," he said. "He has an alibi for both the break-in and the car incident."

"No, that can't be." Kate couldn't believe he wasn't behind all this.

"We verified it, ma'am. He was in the hospital. He's still there, actually."

She simply gaped at the officer, still trying to wrap her mind around the fact their prime suspect didn't do it. Then she registered what Fisk said. "Hospital?"

"Dying, ma'am. Brain tumor."

"That's horrible." Kate digested this bit of unexpected news.

"I guess so."

"Does he know anything about the break-ins or the car ramming us?

"He said he doesn't. But I think he was hiding something. If we learn anything else, I'll let you know."

Kate slumped against the counter. "Thank you, Sergeant." She sighed as the sergeant left. Now what? One step forward, two steps back. It had made perfect sense James Lacey was the man behind everything. Now she had to wrestle with the fact it wasn't him.

She couldn't believe the strong, powerful man who'd intimidated her at the store a few days ago was dying. She gasped as she realized: not just some random man, but her grandfather. The grandfather she didn't even know she'd had was dying. She sat hard on the chair behind the counter and reached for phone, anxious to call Alex, although she knew he was working. It went straight to voice mail. "Alex, it's Kate. James Lacey has an alibi. He couldn't have done it. I don't know what to think now. I was convinced all this drama was over. He's in the hospital, and Fisk said he's dying. He's my grandfather, and that just kind of sank in, so, I think..." she drew in a breath. "Um, yeah, I'm going to take Jupiter home, then I'm going to visit Mr. Lacey in the hospital. Is that crazy? It might be. I don't know. But I'm going to do it anyway. I'll talk to you later."

Silence greeted Kate as she stepped into James Lacey's hospital room. She expected beeps and electrical machines running, but instead a deep quiet draped the room. Mr. Lacey lay in the partially reclined bed, his eyes closed. Should she wake him up or leave? She wanted to leave. She had no clue what to say to him. Setting her purse on the counter, she walked to the window and stared at the cars parked down below while she wondered why she'd come.

"Now that's customer service. You came all the way to the hospital to sell me the Christmas village?"

Kate spun in surprise, then took a few hesitant steps toward the bed, stopping several feet away. "I'm afraid it's too late for that now."

He closed his eyes again. "I'll bounce back from this. I always do."

"Good to know, but it's not what I meant."

"I don't have time for riddles and games, so I suggest you say what you came to say."

"Judith Delaney was my grandmother."

His eyes snapped open and he lifted his head from the pillow to study her. "I didn't know she had a granddaughter."

"Her son was my father."

"That's usually how it works."

"I think that makes you my grandfather."

He leaned his head back against the pillow and sighed. "You found the letters, didn't you?"

"Yes. And the deeds. Is that why you wanted to buy the village?"

"Yes."

"How did you know the letters were there?"

"I didn't. But I thought they might be. When we were young, the plain putz house—the one without decorations—was where she hid her secrets. At first, it was a pretty rock or a candy machine ring. Maybe a love letter or two as she got older. That house was one her father made shortly before he died, so she treasured it and kept it out year-round."

He paused to catch his breath. "I'd heard years ago the entire village was destroyed, but when I saw it in the window of your shop, I knew it was hers. I thought maybe it was still hiding her secrets."

"Why do you think she lied?"

"I'd like to think she had a change of heart about blackmailing me but didn't want to admit it."

His words intrigued her. "What do you mean?"

He didn't answer right away, then he pushed himself up a bit taller in the bed. "She and I dated when we were younger, but I wasn't good enough for her. Poor family, no job prospects. She married that idiot mayor, but, as you know, we kept seeing each other and she got pregnant. I thought this was finally my chance to be with her." He gave an ungentlemanly snort. "But she wanted to protect her so-called marriage. Wanted to tell everyone the baby was his."

He paused to take a few deep breaths, and Kate stepped forward, but a quick shake of his head stopped her. He reached for the cup of water sitting on the table next to him and took a few small sips. "It made me so mad that I threatened to expose her. She gave me the land—you know all this."

"Yes," Kate hesitated, then forged ahead, "but I don't understand the transfer-on-death deed. Why did you give the land back?"

Lacey growled. "Don't bury me quite yet, darling. The land's not yours until I'm dead."

Kate flinched at the sarcasm coating the endearment. "I know. That's not why I'm here. I just want—"

"Answers," he interrupted. "How noble." He rolled his eyes. "I needed some permits I was unlikely to get."

"You gave away five hundred acres for some permits?"

Lacey sneered. "I might have also needed some people to look the other way regarding a few business deals I'd made. Happy now? Anyway, Judith was no dummy and she saw her opportunity. At first, she just wanted money, but we eventually settled on that death deed. I thought it worked out pretty well in my favor. What did I care what happened to the land after I was dead? I had no family at the time."

Kate winced at the disregard for her father.

"And she'd been so high and mighty when I blackmailed her. Turns out it wasn't so beneath her after all." He glanced toward the window for a moment before closing his eyes and laying his head back on the pillow.

He didn't speak for so long that Kate wondered if he'd fallen asleep. Or... was he breathing? She touched his wrist for a pulse.

He jerked his arm from her hand and glared at her. "I'm not dead, granddaughter."

Kate blinked at the venom in his voice and took a step back. "I'm sorry."

He scowled at her before continuing his story. "We agreed to wait to record the death deed in land records. They're public, and we didn't want to risk questions we'd rather not answer. It's effective whether it's recorded or not, and there's no statute of limitations on recording a deed. Her lawyer was supposed to take care of recording it when one of us died, whoever went first. Turns out it was her. I found it rather amusing she never got to reap the benefits of her blackmail." He narrowed his eyes. "But I didn't know about you."

Kate flinched. "And the village supposedly being destroyed?"

"So many questions."

She stiffened. "Look, someone has broken into my store and my home, destroyed my livelihood, then tried to kill me and my friend. So, yeah, I have some questions. And I deserve the answers."

Something flickered in her grandfather's eyes. "Maybe you do," he muttered before clearing his throat. "A few months after she'd passed, I saw her lawyer in town. I'd been checking land records and knew the death deed hadn't been recorded, but I didn't know if it was because the lawyer hadn't gotten around to it, or if, for some reason, he didn't know about it. I asked a few questions, trying to feel him out. Eventually I mentioned the putz houses, and he said the entire village had burned in a fire." Lacey held up a shaky hand. "And before you ask, I don't know why she'd tell him that. I heard she found God or something, but... I like to think she remembered that she used to love me once upon a time." A small smile played on his lips before he schooled his face back to ambivalence. "So now you know, so now you may go."

Kate let out a puff of air in humorless laugh and muttered

sarcastically under her breath. "Ok then." She made her way to the door, then stopped. Gathering her courage, she turned back to him. "If you didn't break into my shop, who did?"

"I don't know."

"Who else would know about that house?" she pressed, certain he did know something despite his assertion to the contrary.

"No one still alive."

"Who else has reason to keep that information hidden?"

"Miss Sinclair, I'm tired. I don't know anything about your problems. It was nice of you to come visit, but I can't help you anymore." He reclined the bed and closed his eyes.

Kate could tell she'd get nothing more out of him. "Good-bye... grandfather." She left the room and walked slowly toward the elevator. Nothing made sense. And Sergeant Fisk was right —her grandfather was definitely hiding something. But what? She pushed the down button harder than necessary and blinked back tears. Could it really be possible that even after all the clues, they were on the wrong track?

Once out of the hospital, she stepped to the side of the automatic front doors. She needed to gather herself before she lost it. She took a couple deep breaths, then began to pray silently.

Help me, Lord, please. I'm so frustrated. I need this to be over. Can you just make it all make sense? Also, I know you're always with me, but I wouldn't mind if you could help me feel it a little more right now. It's hard to wrap my head around the fact that my own grandfather hates me, and someone else wants me dead.

She breathed out an amen and began the two-block walk to the bus stop. She went over all the evidence they'd found. Was there another conclusion? Were they missing something, or putting the pieces together in the wrong way? Arriving at the bus stop, she reached for her purse to pay the fee and found herself searching the air with her hand. Where was her purse? Her shoulders dropped as she recalled a vague memory of setting the bag down in her grandfather's room. With frustration growing, she headed back to the hospital as the bus pulled up behind her.

BACK IN HER GRANDFATHER'S HOSPITAL ROOM, KATE NOTICED THE curtain around his bed had been drawn. She tiptoed to avoid waking him as she eased around the curtain. A man bent over the bed, holding a pillow over James Lacey's face.

She gasped.

The man let go of the pillow and spun to face her. The innocent expression he'd assumed as he turned morphed into an evil smile. She darted towards the door, but he grabbed her arm before she made it out of the room.

"Help!" She yelled, but she wasn't sure anyone would hear her. He shoved the door closed, his grip tightening on her upper arm as he spun her around to face him.

"Kate Sinclair. How nice of you to return. Saved me the trouble of having to track you down."

Kate opened her mouth to scream but he slapped his hand across her mouth, stifling her breath. Before she could recover, he slammed her backwards against the wall. Her knees buckled as her head made contact with the hard surface, but his grip kept her upright. He put his face close to hers and narrowed his eyes. "I'm going to need you to not scream, Kate. I don't want to hurt you, but I will. Do you understand?"

She nodded and he dropped his hand from her mouth.

"Good. It's so much easier to have a civilized conversation this way."

"Do I know you?"

He gave a mocking half bow. "We haven't been formally introduced. My name is John Lacey, and I believe I'm what they call your uncle. Or half-uncle anyway—is that a thing?"

"James Lacey is your father?"

"Was, I believe." He looked at his father with what appeared to be genuine sadness. "I didn't mean to kill him. But he wanted to change his will to include you, and well..." He shrugged. "Crazy old man thought it might keep you quiet, make you more pliable."

Horror at hearing John admit to murdering his father flooded her senses. "You killed him for money?"

"No, nothing so trivial as that." John leaned towards her. "I killed him for a lot of money. But like I said, it was an accident."

"Completely understandable. It was a lapse of judgment."

John frowned and pushed her closer to her grandfather's bed. "Don't patronize me, Kate." He turned to close the curtain behind them, and Kate took the opportunity. She shoved him as hard as she could, then sprinted to the door.

She only managed a couple of steps before a heavy hand hit her in the back, knocking her to the ground. He stood over her as she gasped in air.

"You disappoint me, Kate." He knelt to peer into her face. "But I can see that you're distracted here. I think it's best we go to a quieter place. What do you say?" He pulled a gun from his waistband, racked the slide, and smiled at her. She tried to scramble away from him, but he grabbed her arm and jerked her to her feet.

"If you draw attention to us, things will get messy. I've asked this once before and I don't like repeating myself. Are you going to stay quiet?"

Her eyes on the gun, Kate managed a single nod.

"Good girl. Now we're going to walk calmly out of the hospital." He put the gun in his jacket pocket, keeping his hand on it. With the other hand, he took her arm and nodded to the door.

She opened it and he directed her down the hallway. A few doors down, a doctor talked with a nurse. John whispered in her ear. "I see them too, but remember, if you draw attention to us, what happens to them will be your fault."

Kate shivered. Could he be bluffing? He'd already killed one person—his own father—so he had nothing to lose. She couldn't risk other people's lives, so she kept quiet.

Neither spoke as they left the hospital and headed towards what she supposed was his car. He opened the driver's door, got in, and pulled her after him as he slid across to the passenger seat. He took the gun out of his pocket and pointed it at her. "You're going to drive so I can keep my eyes on you. No funny business. Agreed?"

Her hands shook as she reached for the key in the ignition. She took in a deep breath. *Lord, this really isn't how I expected you to answer my prayer. Help me. And if I fail here, please keep Alex and his family safe.*

She jumped as John tapped the steering wheel with the barrel of the gun. "Take me to the deed."

CHAPTER 20

Alex beat Sergeant Fisk to the hospital's front doors, a prayer looping over and over in his mind—*Dear God, keep Kate safe*. Fisk hadn't told him much on the drive over, but the public record he'd shared included a list of criminal suits longer than a CVS receipt. Alex could tell there was more that Fisk couldn't share and the worry on the officer's face made his stomach clench.

"You really think she's in danger?" Alex punched the up button for the elevator, his gut telling him Kate needed help pronto but his head not wanting to believe it.

"I'd feel better if she wasn't left alone."

The elevator doors opened, and they entered together as Fisk continued. "Lacey's son has a history of violence, not to mention the most to lose if it's discovered he's not the only heir. My search on him revealed a few things that concern me."

"Like what?" Alex willed the elevator to rise faster to the fifth floor and James Lacey's room.

"Let's just say he really needs that inheritance." Fisk tightened his mouth, leaving Alex to fill in the blanks.

As they neared Lacey's room, the hustle and bustle of nurses and doctors entering and leaving the room made Alex even more nervous. Something wasn't right.

A nurse rushed up to Fisk. "Thank goodness you're here. Come with me." Alex followed Fisk into Lacey's room, where the man rested in his hospital bed, his face pale and his eyes wide. A beefy security guard flanked him while a doctor finished an exam of the patient.

"He's lucky to still be alive," one of the nurses whispered to Fisk.

Lacey harrumphed. "Luck would've let me die. That's what I've been waiting for, isn't it?" His eyes shifted to take in Alex and Fisk. "Ah look, the cavalry has arrived."

"What happened?" Fisk directed his question at the security guard.

"Someone tried to smother him with a pillow."

"It wasn't 'someone.'" Color returned to Lacey's face. "It was my son. My own son, that ungrateful—"

"Where is he now?" asked Sergeant Fisk.

"He's gone, the coward. Couldn't even make sure he finished the job." Lacey crossed his arms over his chest, but his breathing was labored, indicating he was more shaken than he wanted to admit.

A nurse spoke to the sergeant. "John probably thought Mr. Lacey was dead, but he'd only lost consciousness. Temporarily."

"The idiot can't even kill someone correctly." Lacey swatted away a nurse who tried to take his temperature with an ear thermometer.

Alex barely held onto his patience. He didn't care about Lacey or the attempted murder—he was here for Kate, and he needed them to focus. "What about Kate?"

"What about her? She's not here." Lacey glared at Alex. "I've got more important things to worry about right now than that woman.

The older man's callous disregard for his own granddaughter brought Alex's blood to the boiling point. He moved toward the bed, but the security guard blocked his path.

"Sir, step back." The guard puffed out his chest. "We are dealing with an attempted homicide here."

"And I'm the law, you moron." Fisk inserted himself in front of Alex. "Mr. Lacey, Kate could be in real danger from your son. He tried to kill you. He might have more success with her."

Lacey sighed. "She was here, but she'd already left by the time John arrived."

Alex clenched his fists at the wasted time. As he surveyed the organized chaos in the room, a bag on the counter caught his attention. He reached for it. "This is her purse!"

"I told you, she was here, but she left," Lacey said.

A nurse briefly touched Alex's arm. "I saw the woman who was visiting earlier come back."

"When?" Alex tried to keep his tone level but wasn't sure he'd succeeded.

"I don't know," the young nurse scrunched up her nose as if trying to recall the exact time, "maybe twenty minutes later."

"John arrived seconds after she left," added Lacey.

"So he'd have been in here when she came back, probably for her purse," Fisk said, his words not making Alex feel any better about the situation.

"But her purse is still here." Alex held it up to remind everyone.

An orderly, his arms full of clean bed linen, came into the room. "Are you talking about the man and woman who left Mr. Lacey's room in an awful hurry?"

Alex's stomach hit the floor. "You saw them? Together?"

The orderly nodded. "Yes, they were walking down the hall towards the exit. They caught my attention because I've seen the man here fairly often, but he's always been alone."

Alex grabbed Fisk's arm. "He's got her." He sprinted out the door, Fisk close on his heels, already calling dispatch to find out what kind of car John drove and to put out an APB to locate it.

Once in the cruiser, Fisk sped out of the parking lot. He slammed his hand on the steering wheel. "I can't believe I didn't catch on to John Lacey sooner."

"You caught it now." Alex willed the man to go faster. "Where are we going?"

Fisk drove towards the heart of town. "I'm not sure—maybe his house, his father's house, an unknown house we know nothing about. We need to figure this out."

"If he doesn't want to kill her—"

"Who says he doesn't?" the sergeant interrupted. "He did just try to kill his father."

Alex's gut tightened. He couldn't about think that right now. John took Kate with him, so he must want something from her. Alex spoke through clenched teeth, "If he doesn't want to kill her… then what does he want?" He snapped his fingers. "The death deed!"

"You're probably right. I didn't see it in land records, so she might have the only copy. He'll have to get it and destroy it, or he loses the property."

"I don't know whether it's at her store or… oh no…"

"What?"

"It could be at my parent's B&B." Alex didn't like the thought of his mom and dad being in danger from someone as deranged as John Lacey sounded. "But I don't think she'd take him there. She wouldn't want to put them in danger."

"Then where would she go?"

"Either her home or the store. It's all she knows."

Fisk reached for his radio. "I'll send officers to both places, as well as the B&B. We'll head to her house. If she's worried about putting others in danger, it's the most secluded choice."

Alex barely listened to Fisk ordering the backup. Instead, he prayed for Kate's safety. He wasn't sure when she'd become so important to him, but he had no intention of losing her now.

CHAPTER 21

On the porch of her house, the gun against her back made focusing on what to do difficult, but Kate needed to think—and she needed more time. She purposely fumbled with the key in the lock of her new door, hoping the angry man behind her wouldn't notice her delay tactics. She'd driven here in as roundabout a way as possible but that hadn't been enough time to formulate a plan to get out of this mess.

John slammed his hand against the door frame. She hated that she jumped in response to his ire.

"Don't think I don't know what you're doing."

She plastered an innocent expression on her face as she glanced at him. "What?"

"I know you didn't really get lost on the way here from the hospital."

"I don't ever go to that side of town. I got turned around." Her protests died on her lips as he moved the gun from her spine to her temple.

"Do. Not. Mess. With. Me."

Her shaking hands made the struggle to insert the key in the lock even more difficult—no need to fake it, she truly couldn't seem to execute the simple task.

He growled low in his throat. "I'll do it myself." Crowding beside her, he unlocked the door, then yanked her in behind him. He slammed the door closed. "I'm done with your games. I want that deed now."

"And then you're going to kill me?" She figured they might as well be clear as to the eventual outcome of this scenario.

He shoved her further into the house. "I already told you." His eyes narrowed to slits. "You get me what I need, and I don't have reason to."

Kate snorted, the sound surprising him into raising his eyebrows. She was surprised by it as well. She didn't know where this newfound composure came from, but she would roll with it. "I don't believe you. I'm a witness. And more than that, you don't want to split your father's inheritance with me. You killed your own father just to have it all for yourself. So if you're going to kill me anyway, I have no reason to help you." She crossed her arms over her chest for emphasis.

"What about your loved ones? I'd hate for harm to come to them."

"You lose again. I have no loved ones."

"Really?" His eyes glowered with malice. "What about that lovely family that owns the B&B in town? And, you've been spending an awful lot of time with that UPS man. Does my niece have a boyfriend?"

Kate stiffened. Why had she allowed Alex and his family to worm their way into her heart and life? Now she'd put them in danger too.

"Maybe I'll leave you alive after all, let you live with what you did to them."

"You're sick," she spat out, anger and fear mingling together in the pit of her stomach.

He gestured with the gun. "Get me the deed, Kate."

"Get it yourself." She had to believe he wouldn't actually hurt Alex and his family. What would be the point after she was dead? All he wanted was the inheritance, and she wasn't going to help him.

"You think I didn't try? I looked all over this house. You obviously have a good hiding place."

"So it was you who broke in to my house. You trashed my store too?"

"Of course." He cocked his head. "Wait, you had someone else in mind? Ooh, who did you think did it? I've got to hear this."

Kate pursed her lips, not wanting to give him the satisfaction. John ran the barrel of the gun down her arm, raising goosebumps in its wake. "C'mon, tell Uncle John. Who was your main suspect?"

She held her ground with effort. "Your father."

John laughed, a rusty sound as if he rarely found life amusing. "Seriously? Old James Lacey? Even in his younger days, he only risked getting his hands dirty when it personally benefited him. The death deed hurts me, not him."

He was letting his guard down. She decided to ask the questions swimming around in her mind to keep him talking. "Why did you wait so long to try to get the deed?"

John shrugged. "I didn't know about it. Dad never mentioned it before. He figured after all this time, it was a non-issue. But when he saw those ugly houses in the window, I think he wondered. He had a bad spell the next day and ended back in the hospital. Thought it was finally the end, so he shared all his secrets. Funny thing about deathbed confessions—they're a little anticlimactic if the person doesn't actually die." John smirked at his own joke. "He didn't know you were a relative, but he knew if that deed was found, it would keep me from inheriting the property. So I decided to not let that happen." John turned serious again. "Finding out you're his granddaughter is an additional complication. But I'm getting tired of all this talk." He prowled around the room. "Where's that dog of yours? Maybe I can use him to motivate you."

"You wouldn't dare!" With his attention still diverted, Kate lunged for him. She managed to get her fingers around the gun, but he didn't let go. In the ensuing struggle, he wrapped his arm around her, the muzzle of the gun now pressed against her stomach. She sucked in air as his arm tightened.

"That was a stupid thing to do." His shout made her ears ring.

"The only reason you're not dead right now is that deed." With a shove, he sent her sprawling on the kitchen floor, the gun aimed at her head. "But then again, if I can't find it, maybe no one else would either. Or should I expand my search to the B&B? What do you think, Kate?" His finger hovered over the trigger, and he leaned down. The cruelty in his voice and eyes terrified her. "Get me the deed, or I kill you now. And anyone else who might get in my way."

The crash of glass breaking caused them both to jump. Kate screamed and dropped to the floor. A black blur streaked across the room and plowed into John, slamming him to the floor and sending the gun skidding away.

Kate focused on the weapon, snatching it up to aim it at John, only then realizing that Jupiter had him pinned to the ground, John's arm in his mouth. The gun shook in her hands, but she kept it trained on John until something touched her arm. She jumped and spun.

"Easy, Kate, it's me. It's Alex."

Alex! His voice made her knees go weak and she allowed him to extract the gun from her hands and set it on the kitchen table. Then he enfolded her in his arms. "Shhh, everything's going to be okay."

She wrapped her arms around him, not planning to let go anytime soon.

"*Aus*! Good boy, Jupiter, *aus*."

Sergeant Fisk had Jup by the collar, tugging the large canine off John, who lay whimpering on the floor.

Jupiter bounded over to Kate, whining and pawing at her until she put her hand on his head. "It's ok, Jup. Good boy."

Fisk handcuffed John and pulled him to his feet. "You okay, ma'am?"

Her face still partially buried in Alex's chest, she mumbled, "Stop calling me 'ma'am,' Sergeant."

"Yes, ma'am." He winked before marching John ahead of him through the shattered back door.

With John gone, questions crowded Kate's mind. "What just happened? How did you know I'd be here?"

"Fisk discovered John's history of violence, and as Mr. Lacey's only child, figured he might be involved since he had the most to lose if the death deed came to light. Fisk wanted you under protection but when he couldn't find you, he called me." Alex smoothed a strand of hair off her cheek. "We went to the hospital—John's attempt to kill Lacey failed—we figured John must have taken you. I knew you wouldn't want to put anyone else in danger, so we guessed that you'd make him think the deed was at your house, away from other people."

"That's good thinking."

"I was doing a lot of praying, so maybe it wasn't all entirely luck."

His confession made her smile. "And Jupiter?" The dog woofed and Kate knelt to bury her face in Jup's neck.

"You mean Jupiter the Wonder Dog?" Alex bent to give Jupiter a well-deserved back scratch. "When we got here, Fisk wanted to sneak around back, which is when we saw Jupiter. I remembered what you said about him being trained as a police dog. Since Fisk knew the German word for attack, we gave it a try."

"But I told you he was a dropout." She rubbed the dog's ears.

"Yes, but it's amazing what someone will do when they're protecting someone they love."

Kate's hand stilled on Jupiter's head. Her heartrate's acceleration had nothing to do with fear this time. "It is?"

Their eyes met. Alex cupped her elbow to help her rise, then enfolded her into his embrace. "Yes, it is."

"It's almost as if you're a hero." She rested her hands on his chest, feeling his heartbeat behind her palm.

"From now on, I just want to be your hero. I'll leave everyone else to Jupiter."

"My gain, their loss."

His arms tightened around her. "No offense to Jupiter, of course."

"Of course." Tired of talking, she moved her hands to the back of his head, applying just enough pressure for him to take the hint. His lips met hers for a brief kiss before he took a step back although he kept his arms around her waist. "Not that I don't want to keep doing this, but are you sure you're okay?"

"With being kidnapped or being kissed?"

"Uh, the first thing."

"I'm alright. Or I will be." Touched by his concern, she decided to be as honest as she could. "I won't lie—I was scared out of my mind. He had every intention of killing me. But that was a spectacular rescue. Thanks to Jupiter and Sergeant Fisk, I'm alright."

"To Jupiter and Sergeant Fisk?" He raised an eyebrow, though there was a twinkle in his eye.

"Oh fine, to you too."

His gaze intensified, the warmth sending shivers down her spine. "And the second thing? You're okay with that?"

Kate leaned back in his arms and shrugged. "You know, I've heard about seeing fireworks when you kiss the right guy, but that didn't really happen."

Alex narrowed his eyes. "It didn't?"

"No." She couldn't keep the grin from spreading over her face. "But I'd swear that I saw Christmas lights."

His laugh wrapped around her, releasing more of the tension in Kate. "Well then, happy holidays to both of us." He dipped his head and his lips met hers again, but this time the kiss didn't end as quickly. His hand moved to the back of her head as he feathered kisses down her jawline onto her neck, causing her breath to skip. Kate leaned in, sliding her hands to his chest. She wrapped her fingers around the front of his shirt and pulled him closer, eliminating what little space was left between them. His mouth found hers once again. Kate reveled in the feel of his lips on hers, not caring one bit that those twinkling lights in her mind were about to blow due to sudden power surges.

CHAPTER 22

On Christmas morning, Kate sat on the couch in the Whitlow home, the stack of her grandmother's photos on her lap. Christmas carols filled the air, and the lights of the Christmas tree brightened the room. To her surprise, she liked it. From ignoring the holiday to enjoying it was an ongoing journey, but she'd come a long way.

Alex plopped down next to her and put his arm across her shoulders. He nodded at the cinnamon roll he handed her. "See, not all Christmas traditions are bad."

"I'm starting to realize that." She took a large bite of the roll. "There are definitely a few I could get behind."

"Oh yeah? Which ones?"

"I liked decorating the tree."

"And the hot chocolate afterward."

"Definitely," she mumbled around another bite of cinnamon roll. She swallowed it before continuing, "and the candlelight service last night was amazing."

"Agreed. Any other traditions worth keeping?"

She tilted her head. "That mistletoe one was pretty good."

"Who needs mistletoe?" He leaned forward, his lips warm on

hers. He lingered there until the moment was interrupted by the twins bounding through the room, Jupiter chasing after them.

Kate winked at Alex then returned her attention to the cinnamon roll and pictures. She dug through the photos until one caught her eye and she stilled, her hand hovering over a photo of a little girl posing with the young woman Kate now recognized as her grandmother. She picked up the picture to study it more closely. The Christmas village, complete with the dark house, was in the background of the picture, set up under a small table-top tree.

Alex nudged her elbow. "What's wrong?"

Kate touched the photo, unable to believe her eyes. "It's me."

"What?"

She held the photo in front of him. "The little girl in the photo. It's me."

"How is that possible? I thought you never met her."

"I didn't think I had. But you know, that village did look familiar the first time I took it out of the box. I feel like I do have some vague memory of it." She flipped the image over to read the wording on the back.

My sweet granddaughter, the only Christmas we had together. I pray for her every day and hope someday we are allowed to be reunited.

"Allowed to be reunited?" she questioned. "Why wouldn't she be allowed to see me?"

Alex re-read the script. "Looks like you have another mystery to solve."

"Hey, Kate." Jessie entered the room and handed Kate a small, wrapped present. "Found one more. From Santa." One of the twins hollered from the kitchen and Jessie hustled out of the room, muttering under breath. "If they're eating more cinnamon rolls, I swear..."

Kate stared at the present. All the gifts she'd received this morning were from the Whitlows as a family. But this one...

Alex whispered in her ear, "Open it."

She tentatively tore the paper and opened the box. When she spied the rawhide bone, she raised an eyebrow.

Alex had a sheepish look on his face. "I honestly didn't know how you'd react if I got you a present, so that's for Jupiter. He's my hero from now on."

"Jupiter will love it. Thank you."

"So next year, if I got you a present...?"

"I think it'd be okay. As long as it isn't a rawhide."

"Deal." His lips brushed hers.

"For this year..." she made sure they had the room to themselves, "I'll take a couple more of those."

"Another Christmas tradition to get behind." Their next kiss unfolded more slowly, causing her heart to do a little jig in her chest. When he finally pulled back, she took a deep breath and let it out on a soft laugh. He brought his forehead to hers. "Merry Christmas, Kate." Then he kissed her again.

If Kate had known how sweet Christmas kisses could be, she might have embraced the holiday sooner. She smiled to herself as she kissed him back.

Merry Christmas indeed.

THE END

ACKNOWLEDGMENTS

I want to thank everyone who supported me in anyway, big or small.

Is that good enough? It's my first published book, so I'm still learning. No? Ok then, read on.

So many thanks to Ann, Elizabeth, Heather, Pam, and Sarah —my previously mentioned writer's group—for their support, encouragement, editing, browbeating, and harassment. Seriously, I'm very thankful for all of that. They believed in me so much they gave their time, energy, brainpower, and even finances to make this book happen. If you didn't like it, blame them.

Thanks to Christine, Gin, Martha, Paula, Susan, and Suzanne for, basically, just existing in my life. They weren't necessarily involved in the writing process, though a couple of them have been my writing cheerleaders and even let me bounce some ideas off them once in a while, but mostly they have listened to me whine and complain, have gone on adventures with me, have shared their families with me, have been a huge distraction from writing (which is honestly needed sometimes, though probably not as often as I used it), have geeked out on history and literature with me, and/or just been a good friend. And I wouldn't do anything productive, much less write a book, without a few good friends. (They are listed alphabetically, so don't read anything into it.)

Thanks to Caitlyn for the photos as well as the support and encouragement.

Thanks to my book club for continually suggesting books that are written so much better than I could ever write and make me feel horrible about myself, while simultaneously making me think, "I could do that." And because, in my opinion, every writer needs some people to talk books with, even if it's not their book. Because writers are readers too, y'all.

Thanks to Kathleen. She knows why.

Thanks to my dad, who really did say the story was "not bad," but also encouraged me and let me work out my plot holes and editing miseries with him.

And, God, for putting this crazy desire to tell stories into my brain, I thank you. I think.

ABOUT THE AUTHOR

Janda Sample lives in Northern Virginia with her cat, Levi. She considers herself a storyteller, not just through writing, but also through acting, directing, photography, and even some editing and sound engineering. She writes mostly romantic suspense, but has also written several plays for her church and a local school, a few short stories and poems, a couple VBS dramas, and a handful of devotionals.

Made in the USA
Middletown, DE
05 October 2023

40182074R00076